IN A VANISHING ROOM

MYSTERIES BY ROBERT COLBY

IN A VANISHING ROOM

ROBERT COLBY

WILDSIDE PRESS

CHAPTER 1

The trouble began when Norris stepped off the plane at Idlewild in New York and the frantic looking girl with the dark red hair spoke to him. She was there at the gate, tiptoe, squinting at the long file of passengers. Norris was among the last to exit and the girl was peering over his shoulder. When her eyes returned empty to settle upon him, he knew she was going to speak. And she did.

That was when the trouble began. Although later Norris concluded that there would have been no reason for the girl to speak to him or anyone else, but for the odd, tense little scene which occurred some three hours earlier at another terminal, the International in Miami from which he had departed.

He was standing with the small cluster of people waiting before the desk to have their tickets checked, their baggage weighed for the loading. He was straddling the big tan suitcase, the unfamiliar hat perched awkwardly on his head, the polo coat over his arm. It had been years since he had worn any sort of topcoat and the frayed polo was all that he had to protect him against the possibility of a sudden chill in the fall air of the North. It seemed inappropriate to arrive at the office of his prospective employer in such a coat, one that would signal a certain desperation. He was worrying about the matter when there was a brush against his arm. The man who had been standing just behind him swooped up a large black case and began to run madly towards the nearest exit, the bag slapping against his thigh and slowing his progress to such an extent that in the end he dropped it altogether and flew out the door.

At first Norris could see no reason at all for the man to be running, let alone with such wild abandon that he discarded his suitcase for still more haste. But then, across the terminal floor, thundering from the other direction, he spied the two big men in the dark suits. They were heavy-jawed, raw-boned, crew-cut blonds with an alien semblance to their features.

They ran after the other in great leaping strides, scattering everyone in their path, each taking a different door to the street.

They were back in less than a minute, apparently unsuccessful. Breathing hard, straightening their clothes, they stared at the curious watchers, picked up the fallen black case and departed.

That seemed the end of it, though Norris held a tableau of the scene in his mind, couldn't shake it for a time. During the first of the flight he puzzled out the possibilities, shading and coloring new pictures of conjecture, all of them sinister, the man pursued gaining his sympathy.

Now he came abreast of the girl waiting at the gate, knowing that she would speak, even guessing the question.

"Are you the last?" she said, touching his arm with long pale fingers which applied a nervous pressure. "I mean, is there anyone else still left on the plane?"

"I'm sorry," he said gravely, for he could see it was a matter of great concern.

"Oh dear." She sighed deeply and he watched the hand fall from his arm with limp resignation.

She was almost as tall as he in her spike heels. Long hair in easy waves. The frail and freckled skin of the true redhead. Green eyes with amber flecks and a full startling blush of mouth. A girl past her mid-twenties with a look of latent animality tightly coiled behind the studied and special veneer of female decorum. She seemed like a graceful panther, which, though zoo-trained and kitten-faced, conceals within itself the atavistic hungers of the jungle.

A girl in jade-green, a sheath without a single embellishment but the lush molding and thrusting of the figure it contained.

"What did he look like?" said Norris who was a man of vast intuitions.

"I beg your pardon?"

"The person you've been expecting. A man, isn't he?"

"A man, yes."

"Would you describe him for me?"

She stared at him curiously, squinting against the declining sun of a brilliant October afternoon. "Why?" she said. "Why do you ask?"

"A rather chunky man," he said. "Not tall, but big in the shoulders and chest. Late thirties, maybe. Dark hair, combed in the middle. A large head—perhaps I should say leonine. He carried a suitcase—black leather, I imagine."

"How did you know?" she gasped.

"It came to me just now. He had to be the one. He stood right behind me in that crush by the ticket desk at Miami International. Just before it happened, my lighter went dry and I asked him for a match. I got a good look at him."

She recoiled as if she had been struck in the face. "Just before *what* happened?"

Norris shifted his weight, feeling strained and uneasy. "Don't worry," he added hastily. "Your friend is perfectly all right. At least, I think so."

"My God," she said irritably, "won't you please tell me about it?"

"Of course," Norris answered, and began. But a giant plane taxiing near smothered his words and he walked her out of range.

"This man is my lawyer," she said. "We had important business. Obviously, he missed the plane."

"That's an understatement," said Norris, smiling broadly for the first time.

"But he is all right?"

"Well…yes. Far as I know. It's quite a story."

"Look," she said, "which way are you headed?"

"The city. About midtown."

"I live on Fifth, near the park. I'll be glad to drive you. Then you can tell me as we go."

"Well, thanks," he said. "I'll have to get my bag. But it won't take a minute."

They began to walk towards the baggage counter. She moved with quick nervous strides, almost leading him.

"I'm Paul Norris." He smiled and waited. Hurrying along now, he glanced at her from the corner of his eye. She was some package! She wore no rings on her fingers. He was excited.

After a moment she said, "Eileen Taggart," mumbling the name absently and without the emphasis of a smile. Her face was drawn and distracted. As well it might be, he thought. Just wait till she hears the rest of it.

Walking to the parking lot, she was silent, fingering keys from her purse. The car was a Jaguar: cream colored and new. She opened the trunk and he hoisted the suitcase. The lid clamped down. They separated and climbed in. He followed lowed her long stockinged legs with his eyes. Down to the shoes—chic, expensive shoes on narrow, clever feet.

She twisted the key and they droned off into an angry swirl of traffic, heading towards Manhattan in the gathering dusk of a day in mid-October.

She leaned back easily, turning slightly towards him, puffing a cigarette.

"Now," she said. "I want you to tell me exactly how it was that Mr. Wheeler didn't catch that plane." Her voice had a tone of command that annoyed him and at the same time made him feel almost guilty, as if he had something to do with it. "Mr. Wheeler is the man you described," she went on. "Harry Wheeler, my lawyer."

Norris delayed. Somehow, because she was such a violent magnet, her attitude irked him still more.

"For God's sake, what's the matter with you?" she snapped. "What happened to Harry?"

CHAPTER 2

It was dark and the city was ablaze with electric fires mounting the sky. Along the avenues traffic moved in the halting rhythm set by the stop lights. The cross streets allowed no rhythm at all. They choked the traffic in their narrow lanes filled with taxis, trucks and escaping commuters.

Seemingly oblivious, Eileen Taggart pushed the Jaguar downtown. In a while she fiddled with the radio, dialing furiously until she found a newscast. Norris was unable to listen attentively. He sat staring at the scene beyond the windshield, trying futilely to get in tempo with the frantic pulse-beat of the city.

Shortly the newscaster's voice was replaced by strident jazz and Eileen cut the radio. "Nothing," she said. "Nothing at all."

"What's that?" Norris flipped his cigarette into the street.

"You're certain he got away?" she said.

"Wheeler? Well, no. I can't be entirely certain. As I told you, it just seemed that he did. Those two characters were back in less than a minute and he wasn't with them. So naturally…"

"They just came back," she said, "and calmly picked up the suitcase?"

"Well, not so calmly."

"How, then? How did they look?"

"Angry. And a little defeated."

"There—you see! He must have escaped."

"I hope so," said Norris. He was merely polite. Perhaps after all, Wheeler didn't deserve his freedom and the men were police. "Of course there's one more possibility," he continued.

"Yes?"

"Another of those men outside. And he held your friend in a car. Something like that."

"No," she said positively. "Because why should they send two men for the suitcase when one could do the job?" Traffic paused for a light. She found a tiny gap in the front line and grabbed the space with a deft maneuver.

"True," said Norris. "I agree." She sounded so cool. Apparently this Wheeler's value to her was not emotional. He was pleased in the way of a male who likes to see all attractive women unencumbered.

Covertly he studied the velvet sweep of her mouth, the soft shadowed rise of her chin. "Don't you have any idea, Eileen? May I call you that?"

"Why not?"

"Don't you have any idea who those men could be?"

"Not even a guess."

"Or what they were after?"

"No. It's a complete mystery. Awful! My God, my God. It's…it's frightening. Harry was never mixed up in anything that I knew of. To me he's just a competent lawyer and a friend. Nothing unusual about him."

"He wasn't carrying anything valuable?"

"Heavens, no. Not for me, at least. Just a divorce agreement, a settlement. Papers to read and discuss, that's all. He was to meet another client here tomorrow. But he didn't give me any details."

"Divorces can be messy," Norris said, "and sad. I'm just recovering from one myself. When is your ordeal?"

"It's over," she said. "Long ago. This was only a change in the financial arrangement."

"I see."

He didn't want to cross-examine her. Rather, he didn't want to give that appearance. He grew silent.

In a moment she said, "This whole thing is so depressing."

"Sure. It would be."

"I don't know what to do. Suddenly I feel lonely and afraid."

"If there's any way that I can help…"

"I don't know how, exactly. But you're very kind, Paul. Where do you stay here in town?"

"I don't. Haven't been to New York in years. Miami is my home, or rather was. You see, I'm changing jobs. I'll pick up a hotel room until I get organized."

"Week nights you can get a room most anywhere, anytime. Do it later. But first stop by my place and have a drink."

Again she was practically ordering. But now he hardly noticed.

"Sure," he said. "I'd like that."

"You won't misunderstand?"

"Of course not." Christ! There it was. The sex defense. But sometimes they meant just the opposite—very often—

"It's only that I'd rather not be alone for awhile."

"I understand that perfectly, Eileen." In truth, he was wretchedly lonely himself. He had no friends in the city. He would lie in his room and he would think back. Think and think. The first night would be a horror. But now this was fine. Instant Company. Female brand. The best.

"When we get to your place, Eileen, why don't you call this Harry Wheeler and see if he got home safely."

"I will. I'll do that first thing."

"Then, if you can't locate him, I really think you ought to contact the police. In Miami, that is."

She swung right and pushed across town. Soon she was blocked behind a patchwork of straining vehicles.

"What on earth would I tell the police?" she said with a spastic tapping of her cigarette over the little tray. "A secondhand story about a chase in the Miami terminal?"

"You don't believe me?"

"Oh, certainly. But would they? The police?"

"I don't know."

"And would they *do* anything about it?"

"Probably not unless he was missing a day or two."

The light changed and they crawled to the intersection.

"Oh, it's…it's simply astonishing," she said. "About Harry. Just insane!"

"Yes," he answered. "Fantastic."

CHAPTER 3

The elevator ascended, made a cushioned stop on fourteen. The man in the crisp green uniform held the door and smiled pleasantly at Eileen Taggart. They stepped off and moved down the corridor to 14 A. Eileen turned the key and Norris followed her into the apartment as she gave it light and closed the door.

The living room was wide and deep with wine-red wall-to-wall carpeting. It was elegantly furnished in subdued modern. There were heavy drapes and rich paintings. Even the little things—ash trays, bowls, vases and figurines—were gems of extravagance, mute symbols of money.

"Charming," said Norris.

"Thank you," she replied. "It's a little large for me alone. But I had grown to love it, and after the divorce I couldn't bear to leave. My husband was quite gracious about it."

Norris stepped across the spongy carpet to a window. Along the dark ribbon of Fifth Avenue below, traffic wheeled with a soundless sparkling. Beyond, the park was a great sprawling shadow laced with dim networks of light.

"What's your ex-husband's line of work?" said Norris, turning to find her standing just behind him, flaming a cigarette.

She exhaled sharply, weighing a table lighter in her palm. "Oh, he's president of a holding company. They buy up different concerns here and there—all of them in trouble. Maybe one has been mismanaged, or another's going under with debts."

"Then what?"

"This holding company puts in new management. And a fresh supply of cash. They set the crippled business on its feet. And when it begins to show a nice profit, they sell it. Usually. Sometimes they hold on. Depends on the situation. But I only like the results. The rest is a bore. Why don't you sit down, Paul? Here, let me take your coat."

"Don't bother," he said, not wanting her to get a closer look. He draped the coat over a chair, placed his hat on top and sat down.

She lifted one eyebrow quizzically.

"Drink?" she said.

"Definitely."

"I have champagne, Scotch, bourbon, almost anything. I make superb Manhattans."

"I'm crazy about superb manhattans."

She flicked her tongue at him, set the lighter on a coffee table and crossed the room. He followed the long concavity of her back, the high buttocks moving in a tight rhythm beneath the sheath. And he thought, I'm only a stand-in for a guy named Wheeler. Any other night she'd be a busy signal. Just lucky—Wheeler pulled the handle and I hit the jackpot. He smiled. Now and then, when you weren't looking, life delivered a neat surprise package.

She opened double doors and revealed a small ebony bar. She made mixing sounds and in a minute brought him a double Manhattan in a champagne glass. He sipped while she fussed over the cabinet of a hi-fi player, burnished red hair spilling down, quick fingers sorting platters.

Music drifted around the room, as if coming forth from a half dozen speakers. Norris lifted his glass. The drink was excellent—a warm interior caress which dispelled his emptiness. He would not think again of the past. It was always better to live hard on the moment, coasting along on whatever waves of chance excitement carried him through the days and nights of his life.

"I must place that call," said Eileen Taggart, over her shoulder, moving away. "I won't be a moment."

"Luck," said Norris, raising his glass. She left the room and distantly there was the *ka-lump* of a door closing.

She returned as Norris set the glass on the coffee table—empty. You were not supposed to gulp a Manhattan and now he would drink slowly. The first quick drink was for relief of tension. Too much had happened too fast.

Eileen brought the cocktail shaker and set her glass beside his on the table. She filled them both and, frowning, sank upon a sofa near him.

"He wasn't there?" said Norris.

She shook her head. "No answer at his home. I had the operator ring a couple of other places. No one had seen him."

"Try not to worry, Eileen. Not yet, anyway. It's early. The man's got trouble and he's busy. He'll phone you at the first opportunity."

She brightened. "That's true. He's certain to call me when he can. He could be in the air, on a later plane."

"Maybe he did call," said Norris. "And he missed you."

"In that case, he'll phone back. I'll just have to wait here. Do you mind?"

Inwardly he smiled. "I have no plans, Eileen."

"I suppose you're ravenously hungry."

"Oh, not very," he lied.

"I'm afraid I have nothing much to offer you. Harry was taking me out to dinner and I—"

"Sure." He waved off her apology. "Besides, I never enjoy drinking on a full stomach. Later, we could have something sent up."

She smiled her appreciation.

He watched her as she plucked her glass from the table. A really startling redhead. Delicious! And the situation was positively unique. No smoky night club for them. No cramped and noisy den until 2 A.M., followed by a mile-long check and then a kiss-off at her door. Rather, they were trapped, by a telephone which might never ring, into this cozy confinement, this cloistered intimacy fraught with marvelous possibilities.

He drank deeply.

An hour later, perhaps two (he had lost track of time), they had removed their shoes and were embracing in time to the sensual beat of a dreamy lament. And though the music was sad, Norris felt weightless and amused. Each time they passed a lamp he reached under the shade and with a quick sly movement, extinguished it. At first she pretended not to notice. But then, after he had erased all but a single light and was peering down at her with a smile twitching his lips, she began to chuckle. He joined her in a duet of laughter. The whole thing seemed enormously funny.

They fell upon the sofa, and still giggling she poured another drink from the shaker on the table. How many was that? Six, seven?

Who cares! There were things to forget and Norris was going about it with energy. He was not really tight, he told himself. It was just that you got a little stoned on an empty stomach. Actually, he felt in charge: dominant; articulate. Though at times his tongue fell behind the racing of his thoughts and he had to begin again with more careful enunciation.

On the sofa, where only the palest of lights reached from the shadows, he made an attempt to pull Eileen closer.

"Careful of my drink, sweetie," she said with a nod at the glass in her hand.

"Toss it down and it won't be in the way, then." He felt a sudden rebellion against all the pretexts of the female. "Excuses," he said sullenly.

She sipped and placed the glass carefully on the table. "What excuses?" She tossed her hair and smiled, her lips moist and provocatively close.

He tried to kiss her. She ducked and made a teasing sound in her throat.

"Women," he said disgustedly.

"What about women, Paul? Tell me all about women."

"They learn the game around fifteen and they're still playing it at fifty. You'd think even *they* would get bored."

"What game, Paul?"

He knew she was baiting him but went on anyway. "Sex checkers," he said. "I move here and you move there. About the third or fourth play, you let me take you. Provi—providing, of course, the stakes are right and you can lose gracefully. All the bright vir—virtues still shining and unsullied."

He smiled, knowing that he was right but aware that he was becoming angry, making a childish and fruitless issue of the thing. With ninety-eight percent of all women, directness was a fatal mistake.

"I ought to go," he said. "I'm getting too…" He trailed off. The point he was making got lost, then returned. "I'm too loaded to be much fun. How 'bout tomorrow night?"

He tried to get up, fell back. He shoved and this time he made it, though as he stood peering down at her, he weaved slightly.

She took his hand and pulled him back beside her. "Paul," she said earnestly. "You're right. About the sex checkers. I was only teasing you. Women are awful bitches. Why don't you stay awhile longer? All right?"

She kissed him then. Violently. With stabbing tongue and gaping mouth, her lips swarming over his, rotating, hungry.

He felt one giant surge of passion as his hand touched her breast, moved on, searching around the tight dress. But then a sick dizziness overcame him and he couldn't work the zipper. His fingers were awkward and ineffectual.

In a haze he watched her rise and remove the dress. And then the slip, and the bra. How carefully she laid them on the arm of the sofa. How he envied her that precise control which he had lost.

She came towards him, wearing only the pale yellow panties. Her breasts were tapered gourds bursting outward, the nipples pink as a Florida sunset.

He stretched back limply on the sofa, more of necessity than desire. Unsmiling and intent, she lay down beside him and pressed close. His arms went around her. His hands groped over her back, then fell away. It was ridiculous. It was absurdly ironic. But his eyes had closed and he was falling asleep. He couldn't, just couldn't prevent it.

In a moment he felt the small pressure of her hand on his brow, fingers kneading. He sank deeper towards sleep. Her body moved, she eased away, and was gone. At the closing edge of consciousness he was touched by regret, and humiliation. She would never forgive him. With a supreme effort he forced his eyes open and turned his head.

He couldn't see her, but heard a faint rustle of movement. He sat up slowly, looking towards the sound. Then his eyes found her in the dusky room.

It seemed impossible that more than a minute had passed. But she was fully dressed, and was bent over something. Now she held it aloft. His coat—the faded polo—why? He saw but still didn't understand. Her fingers were flying at the pockets. They came up with papers—answers to letters of application which he had taken to read on the plane. Why would she want them?

She carried the envelopes to the light and examined them inside and out with frenzied haste. She appeared not to find what she sought.

Her face tightened. She crossed to the coat and went through it again.

He watched, fascinated to see what she would do next.

In a moment she returned the letters to a side pocket and tossed the coat aside angrily. She stepped silently towards the front door.

"What the hell?" he shouted.

She turned, startled.

"Wasn't it in the coat, Eileen? Where to now?"

She flung the door open and slammed it behind her.

He leaped after her. But the hall was vacant.

He went back and ploughed into his shoes. He grabbed the coat and hat and flew out of the apartment.

Down on the street he couldn't find her. But then he saw the Jaguar, and she was in it, rocketing from the curb, lost in traffic, swallowed in the maw of night.

And though he couldn't imagine why it would be of any use to her, his suitcase was in the trunk.

CHAPTER 4

In twenty minutes he had made a room-to-room search of apartment 14A. All the closets, drawers, and cupboards were empty. He could not find so much as a letter, not a scrap of paper in a wastebasket. The kitchen contained utensils, plates, silverware and glasses—all these of the finest quality, the silver sterling. The refrigerator was operating, there were trays of ice and the interior was sparkling clean. But the racks contained not a particle of food. In the living room, the bar was stocked to a rich man's taste. More than half the supply was composed of costly imports.

Norris sank into a chair, holding his head and pressing his throbbing temples. Nausea threatened him. But, if nothing else, he was cold sober.

Obviously it was planned. Everytime he picked up his glass, somehow it was full. While she sipped, pretending to match him, he had downed better than a half dozen Manhattans on an empty stomach!

And from the very beginning, she had wanted to get her hands on that coat. The little scene at the airport was a farce. She was not, had never been, waiting for the one she called Harry Wheeler. She was there for the express purpose of meeting Paul Norris! A subtle and clever act played entirely for his benefit.

Why? he thought. A total stranger. Why? Best not to cloud his logic by imagining some complicated intrigue which involved him. There had to be a simple explanation. Begin with the coat—that was the key—and figure backwards. To the Miami terminal…

It didn't take a minute to come up with the answer. The chunky man with the leonine head, Wheeler, was in a tight spot. He must have seen the two alien-faced blondes approaching, still far off across the immense terminal floor. He knew them—and what they wanted. Something in his possession, whatever that something was, he had to get rid of it quickly!

Wheeler thinks fast. The man in front of him has just been glancing at a ticket for the same nonstop plane to New York. There is only one at this hour. Even if Wheeler missed the ticket, he saw the coat. People do carry coats if they are traveling from one warm climate to another. And anyway, the jam at the desk is comprised of New York passengers.

So instantly Wheeler decides. He drops something into the pocket of the coat which the man in front of him carries over his arm—likely the object is small—and it certainly must have been—likely the man will not notice it. Probably he will not have reason to reach into his pocket during the flight. In any case, one must gamble when the chips are down. The object falls lightly into the pocket of the polo coat, Wheeler picks up his bag and runs. He's lucky. He escapes.

Then what? Immediately, he phones Eileen Taggart in New York. He tells her the story, gives her a description of the man. She drives out to Idlewild, places herself strategically and corners her unwitting delivery boy, Paul Norris. She's a sensational man-trap, and it's a small problem.

But what if Wheeler had been captured and was not able to contact Eileen Taggart? Then Norris comes into possession. And that's bad—for Wheeler. Or is it? Perhaps the article has no value to anyone else. Or maybe Wheeler knows he will be released if the article is not found on his person and thus he will still have time to call.

The odd thing was that Norris did reach into the coat pocket during the flight. For the letters answering his job applications. He had even figured his finances on the back of one. Yet he had found nothing in the coat but the envelopes. Of course he was not looking for anything else. But Eileen was…

Norris picked up the coat and went over it systematically, checking for holes in the pockets. He sorted the letters. All there. He took each letter out of its envelope and shook it. Nothing. Still, he had the feeling of having missed something. Sure! Where was the envelope on which he had penciled those figures?

He remembered! There had been one blank envelope among the others. He had been distracted. Deep in thought, worried. The envelope was clean and so light, he thought it was empty. One of his own that got mixed with the replies. Absently he had used the face of it to figure his budget, supporting the envelope with a magazine. Then he had folded it and…

He reached into his handkerchief pocket, pulled the handkerchief out and felt underneath. He came up with the envelope. It was folded three times. Nervously, he spread it open on the table. It looked thin, innocuous. Just an envelope with his scrawl of figures. But it was, after all, sealed.

Containing his excitement, he tore the flap carefully and looked in. A small piece of light paper, folded in half. He was disappointed. So much fuss and it couldn't be anything much. He plucked the paper and opened it.

MORGAN VAN LINES, INC.

2748-H

Local & Long Distance Moving by Experts
Packing and Storage Warehouses in principal cities
1 crate— Contents—household goods, misc.
Weight—346 lbs.
Hold for delivery

The receipt was signed. It was filled out under the name Harry Wheeler, Miami address. It was marked as prepaid, and the location of a storage warehouse on the west side was given.

Norris was only a little less disappointed. Household goods! Miscellaneous. Yet, much could be concealed under the classification of household goods. The crate could contain almost anything. And probably it held a secret which was worth a fortune to someone.

Well by God, he had been tricked and used and he would find out. Damn right! He would discover that secret.

Now he reached for his wallet and opened it. He checked the cash. Two hundred and sixty dollars. All there. His total reserve against the panic of poverty. Well, at least she had not stolen his money. She was after much bigger game.

Household goods, miscellaneous. 347 pounds. A myriad of conjectures hurried through his mind. And then he thought, Too much weight for a body. But surround the body with junk and add the heft of the crate…. He shuddered.

It occurred to him that he might remain in the apartment all night waiting for her return. But would she come back? Why should she?

Since the place was empty and since he might have called the police, nothing here for her but trouble. Yet when she opened the suitcase and didn't find the receipt—without which, claiming the crate would be close to impossible—what would she do then?

If he stayed all night he would save the expense of a hotel room. On the other hand, he wouldn't sleep a wink, and in the morning he had to report for an interview. But he should be rested and make a good impression.

In the bedroom he found a phone book and looked up hotels. He dialed several in the midtown area which he knew to be reasonable by New York standards. He made a reservation at the one which offered the best rate.

Finally, on the envelope which contained the receipt, he wrote down the number of the phone in apartment 14A.

The elevator descended with a nearly inaudible murmur. For a moment Norris contemplated the narrow back and long neck of the operator.

"Been here long?" he said.

"What's that, sir?" The man turned.

"I mean, have you been working in this building a long time?"

"Seems long, sir. Couple of years."

The elevator came to rest, the door opened.

"What's your name?" said Norris.

"Sir?"

"What do they call you?"

"Henry. Just Henry."

"Cigarette?" Norris extended the pack.

"Not supposed to smoke, but…"

Norris winked and Henry took the cigarette and accepted a light. He inhaled with a sheepish grin.

"Tell me, Henry, how long have the Taggarts had their apartment here?"

Henry frowned. "What was that name, sir?"

"Mrs. Taggart. In 14A."

"No Mrs. Taggart in 14A. No, sir. Place belongs to Mr. Kavanagh. Everett T. Kavanagh. Yes, sir, Mr. Kavanagh, he spends most of his time in Florida. That's where he is now."

"I see. And Mrs. Kavanagh?"

Henry cupped the cigarette in his hand, peered out sharply from the door, ducked in again. "Ain't no Mrs. Kavanagh. Least, not anymore. She died some time ago."

"And the young lady who uses Mr. Kavanagh's apartment?"

"Which one, sir?"

Norris kept a poker face with difficulty. "The one who went up there with me awhile ago."

"Henry looked embarrassed, studied the tip of his cigarette. "Well, sir, you'll pardon me, but I guess you know more about her than I do."

"I don't understand, Henry."

"Well, I seen her just once before. Months ago. Though some people I don't easily forget. She come up to wait for Mr. Kavanagh, had her own key. Never got to know her name."

"Natural enough." Norris spoke casually. "I suppose Mr. Kavanagh has quite a few women friends who use the place?"

"Oh, yes sir. A few. Off and on. Mr. Kavanagh, he has fine taste, really fine!"

"But you don't get to know any of them?"

"No, sir. There's hardly time." He chuckled. "And anyway, we mind our own business here. If Mr. Kavanagh lets a young lady have a key to his place, that's entirely his affair."

"Well, after all, Mr. Kavanagh's an important man, Henry. Isn't that so?"

"Certainly is. A big man. President of his own company."

"Holding company, isn't it?"

"What sort?"

"Holding. They buy up other outfits on the rocks and make them tick like a new watch."

"Yeah." Henry smiled. "Something like that. So I hear. What I know about big business you could put in your eye and not feel it."

Norris stepped off the car.

"Well, nice talking to you, Henry."

"Sure thing. And thanks for the butt."

Norris moved away, then turned back.

"Say, Henry, would you do me a favor?"

"I could try."

Norris took one of the envelopes from his pocket, tore off the back flap and wrote. He handed the paper to Henry.

"That's my name, and there's the phone number of the hotel where I'm staying."

"Yes, sir. You're Mr. Norris."

"Right."

"Now—the young lady, the redhead, may come back tonight. I'm not sure. But if she does, I'd like to get in touch with her." Norris took out his wallet and held it loosely in his hand. "So, if she comes in, you do me a big favor and call me at the hotel any time of the night or morning, it doesn't matter." He took out a five and Henry accepted it with a proper show of reluctance.

"I go off at three," he said.

"If she doesn't show by three, you can forget it, Henry. And I mean forget it. In fact, you're not to mention this little arrangement to the lady at all." He winked. "Understand?"

"Sure, I get it." Henry winked back.

"Good night, Henry. And much obliged."

"Any time, Mr. Norris."

Paul Norris left the building. He could ill afford the five. But it might prove a good investment.

CHAPTER 5

Norris paid the clerk in advance for one night. He explained that his bag would arrive the following day. But he might never see the suitcase again. Then it might cost him about two hundred dollars to replace the clothing alone.

Goddam that bitch! He'd take it out of her hide if he ever caught her.

The bellhop brought him one of those hotel kits—miniature shaving equipment, a toothbrush and paste. Thank God for small favors.

He took a bath and lay on the bed in his shorts, wide-eyed and thoughtful. In the morning, all things being equal, he might actually begin on the new job at Hoffman, Lewis and Pearson. And presently he was in one hell of a state of mind for the sort of concentration required. Yet he must put all else aside. For the job was paramount. Without it he would be broke in three-weeks time, alone and defeated in a city where a stranger had only one friend—the dollar.

And that would be a really pathetic situation for a man who was grossing a hundred seventy-five bucks every five work days in Miami, where he was account executive for the Miami branch of H, L & P. Damn good money in the south. The equivalent opening in New York would pay another fifty. But the increased cost of living would chew it up.

He didn't want to be in New York in the first place, never would have been forced to leave Miami, if not for Carol. She had pulled down the whole neat structure with four words—"I want a divorce."

Norris suffered more than the crush of his ego. They had been married eight years, the first of them pretty much a rat-race on a sloppy track; the handicaps shared with that mutual good spirit which unties under pressure and makes the weld seem inviolate. He had sailed into the ad agency business with both fists, moving up, falling back, shoving ahead again. There had been a hundred problems in every category—ridiculous, annoying, important. But never had he looked in the direction of the real trouble, never had reason to doubt that Carol was the one solid anchor of his life. And when she told him, it was like going to his savings bank—that unshakable bulwark of security—to find the doors locked and a sign reading, *Closed. Out of Business. This Space for Rent.* Except that you could sue for money owed, never for the recovery of affection.

For a time he reasoned. Then he pleaded. And threatened. In the end, he gave up, salvaging some pride, some self-respect. He wanted to hate her. And on the surface, did. But underneath, with cruel persistence, the tortured fragments of needing and loving remained.

He moved out. He drank, savagely, destructively. He escaped in cheap thrills with dyed blondes and vapid brunettes. His work slipped. He arrived hungover and late. Sometimes not at all. He was warned, given a month to "shape up." But he didn't care.

Once drunk and melancholy, he called Carol. And mumbled over and over, "Why? Why, Carol? Why, why, why?" It was a mistake. Because this one time, she was kind. He almost cried. And had to hang up.

When he didn't improve at H, L & P, they put him on notice. In desperation, he made a frank admission of the causes behind his conduct. He asked to be transferred to the New York office, and was told that New York ran its own show, hired its own men. However, he could apply and they would recommend him. But the New York office was staffed. He had to wait.

Meanwhile he sent letters to other companies. The replies were negative, or luke warm.

Then Bill Fowler, a vice president from the home office flew down. He brought news that New York was expanding and they were going to hire another account man. He liked Norris, said the word on him was good. He would talk him up in New York. Nothing to do but sit still for the okay.

In a week Fowler sent Norris a letter to come ahead. The job was his, though he would have to pass an interview with Mr. Hoffman, which was merely formality.

Well, that was a break, because he would have been finished in Miami. In truth, they only wanted to get rid of him, and he couldn't blame them.

But now tomorrow he would see Fowler, and then Hoffman. He would be, in a sense, restored. Though not quite. Not deep within himself. Not for a long time.

He got to sleep, finally, then the phone rang. He thought it was the elevator boy—Henry. But it was only the operator telling him it was eight in the morning. Had he slept seven hours? He felt more like the short end of two. Thanks to Eileen Taggart and her sneaky Manhattans.

Eileen Taggart. Where was she now? Nothing came from Henry, so apparently she didn't show. He got out the phone number of Kavanagh's apartment. He placed the call. No answer. Goodbye suitcase. A trade? One crate for a tired suitcase.

He shaved closely and took special care with his grooming. Dressed and ready, he studied himself in the mirror. The suit was a little rumpled in the back, but otherwise he looked almost prosperous. Now erase that sad-hungry look from the eyes. Make the face bright and alert, but not too eager. That's it! Then he was on his way....

CHAPTER 6

Bill Fowler's secretary, Miss McNeal, was quite obviously pregnant. It amused Norris to think that they still called secretaries "Miss" when they were practically in labor. Miss McNeal was, anyway, rather slight, so that her condition was exaggerated. She had short dark hair, blue eyes and a wistful baby face which belied office efficiency. Her desk sat just outside Fowler's office, the door to which was open, revealing a cluttered desk and an empty swivel chair.

"You're Miss McNeal, aren't you?" said Norris.

"That's right, sir."

"I'm Paul Norris from the Miami office."

"Glad to know you," she said. Her smile was warm.

"Mr. Fowler said you'd find him for me. I have an appointment at ten."

"At ten," she repeated. "Yes, he told me." Miss McNeal looked slightly pained. "The thing is, Mr. Fowler's in conference. And I'm terribly afraid he's going to be tied up all day. Something urgent with a new client. He was awfully sorry. He said perhaps you'd phone him first thing tomorrow."

Norris was annoyed. It looked as if they were going to shuffle him around at their convenience like some forty-a-week office boy down from Backwoods U. Nevertheless he placed a tepid smile on his face.

"Well, that's—that's perfectly all right. Of course I am here from Miami, you know."

"I know," said Miss McNeal. "That's the hell of it. Excuse me."

"Not at all. That *is* the hell of it. How about Mr. Hoffman? Think I could get in to see him? Mr. Fowler was merely going to make the introductions."

"Golly, no! You'd have less chance cornering Hoffy." She bit her tongue. "He's in the same conference."

"I see. Okay then. I'll buzz in the morning." Make it sound breezy.

"And thanks a lot, kiddo."

"For nothing," she said.

He was about to turn away when he caught something shadowed on her face. Something speculative, uncertain, as if hesitantly, she reached out to hold him.

"Was there something else, Miss McNeal?"

"Listen," she breathed, crooking her finger to indicate that he should draw closer.

"Yes?"

I'm leaving this joint. Next week. I'm going to have a baby."

That certainly was no secret. He didn't get the point. "That's nice," he said. "I'm glad for you."

"I'm not coming back, afterward."

"Oh? Sorry to hear it."

"So I just don't give a damn anymore. I mean, I'm on *your* side."

"You are?"

"Yes. And I'm going to tell you something. It's none of my business. None at all. And I have no right... But I feel sorry for you, Mr. Norris."

"You do?" He shifted uncomfortably. "Well, I appreciate—"

"There's no reason why you should be kept standing around on one leg when Hoffy—he's such a big phony—has already filled the position. The account exec thing."

"He what?"

"That's right. Yesterday. Now you won't storm around and embarrass me if I tell you the rest of it, will you?"

"No." His face felt drained. "No, I wouldn't do that to you." He leaned heavily against her desk.

"Well..." She licked her lips. "Mrs. Hoffman has a brother. And the brother has a son. And the son works in the advertising department of a newspaper. And he thinks he knows all about handling big accounts. And so naturally—"

"Naturally!" snapped Norris. "So the son got the job. It's finished. The end."

She sighed. "Mrs. H. has a lot of influence with old Hoffy. And he's the senior partner."

"Oh, the bastards. The bastards!"

"I'll drink to that."

"Jesus, God. Why didn't they let me know before I came all the way up here to New York?"

"Because no one told that gink the job was open until yesterday. Then he hopped right on it. Mr. Fowler was furious. Simply furious! He tried to reach you. But it was too late. He's a very kind-hearted man, Mr. Fowler. Very."

"Then why isn't he here to tell me?"

"You know, I think he would be, in spite of the conference. I think he just couldn't face it, he was that upset. He told me he would pay your plane fare, if it had to come out of his own pocket. He said, just thank the good Lord you had a job to go back to. Otherwise he didn't know what he'd do."

Norris had to smile. That was the biggest joke of all. He wouldn't go back if he could.

"You're a very nice person," he said, "to tell me."

"Oh, no. I didn't have much to lose."

"I hope you and the baby and all are very happy."

"Thanks a lot. You'll pretend to Mr. Fowler, when you call him, that you're still in the dark, won't you?"

"Sure. If I call him."

"I think you ought to. He would worry."

"I'll bet."

"And so would I. Besides, there's the plane fare. You've certainly got it coming."

"Well, look, I'll call him tomorrow. For your sake, anyway. And now I'm going to run before I start breaking the furniture."

She held out her hand and he took it. She squeezed.

"I'm sorry," she said. "Really."

"Goodbye," he said. "And thanks."

In the lobby of the hotel he paused at the entrance to the bar. He was tempted to get very drunk. When the gods fell on you, they devoured you in three great chunks—one chunk at a time, until you were bone-clean. Nothing left of you. Not so much as a morsel of spirit for the vultures of the soul.

But even if he would allow himself to get drunk, he couldn't afford it now. He passed on to the elevator and rose to his floor.

He saw it the minute he opened the door. His suitcase. Standing innocently at the foot of the bed. He heaved it up and opened it. There was rearrangement, but as far as he could tell, everything was there. And pinned to the lapel of his brown suit, was a note. He grabbed it and read.

Sorry. About the suitcase. I had it sent over.

If you have something which belongs to me, I think we should discuss it. I'm sure we could deal. I would make it exceedingly worth while for you to turn over that paper to me.

Could you use a thousand dollars?

Wait in your room for a call. I'll keep trying.

E. T.

She must have believed the receipt was in the suitcase. That's why she raced off in the Jaguar. Probably she brought the case over herself. With some fast talking and a big tip, she could have come up with the bellhop, pretending she was going to wait in the room. Then she could have made a search.

He moved about, inspecting the room. Since there was nothing of his for her to disturb, there was no evidence she had been there. But how could she know where he was staying! Henry? Perhaps. But Norris didn't think so. Henry wasn't the type to play both sides. He had neither guile nor imagination.

He tried the Kavanagh number again. He let it ring ten times and hung up.

A thousand dollars! A lot of money anytime. But when you were nearly broke and without a job…. Damn right he could use a thousand. And because he had been given a rough time by these characters he might take it. Funny thing. Because if she had told him the truth in the beginning, he would have given her the receipt for nothing. Oh, he would have been mighty curious and he would have asked some questions. But in the end, with a fairly logical story, she could have had the paper. He wasn't goong to keep anything which didn't belong to him. People like Eileen Taggart and Harry Wheeler must be operators. They dealt off the bottom. And it never would occurr to them that someone else might play it straight.

As a matter of fact, if the receipt was worth a thousand, it was worth more. It would be amusing to see just how much more.

The phone rang in less than an hour. It was Eileen Taggart.

"Did you find my note?" she asked.

"Of course. How did you know what hotel?"

"Brilliant thinking. I called over a dozen and asked for you by name."

"Clever. Oh, you're a clever one, Eileen. What do you hear from Everett Kavanagh?"

"Beg your pardon? I don't understand."

"Sure you do."

"Well—have you got that paper I want?"

"The receipt? Certainly."

"When can I have it?"

"How much is it worth?"

"Don't be cute. I mentioned a thousand in my note."

"Make it five thousand, no questions asked."

"I'm laughing."

"Not very loud."

"Look, darling, you're wasting your time, and mine. Give up, sweetie. I've got your number. Second-rate hotel, two worn suits and a shabby coat, and you're hunting for a job. You'll take a thousand and like it! Nice try, though."

"You forgot about my pride. It's expensive. Now you've damaged it beyond repair. Also, you searched my suitcase, and my pockets. Highly illegal. Three thousand."

"No. What good is the receipt to you, unless you steal other people's property. Do you?"

"Do you?"

"There are other ways, Paul dear. It would be a lot of trouble. But Harry could prove ownership without the receipt. Or he could uh... persuade you to part with it."

"Is that a threat? The price is going up. Tell you what. We'll go down together and claim the crate. You let me see what's inside, and it won't cost you a penny."

She laughed humorously. "You're terribly funny. But I'll satisfy your curiosity so we can get on with this. The crate contains a valuable painting. Those men were trying to steal it from Harry. So naturally, he put the envelope in your pocket."

"Naturally. And then he called you to charm it away from me."

"I'm sorry. But you understand—now."

"Sure. A painting. A rather large one. Weight—347 pounds. Is it a painting or a monument?"

"There are some other things, household junk, surrounding it and, of course, the crate itself."

"Of course. Why didn't I think of it? So I'll take the receipt to the police department and let them decide what to do with it. Probably they'll open the crate and then—"

"Two thousand," she said. "My last offer. We have nothing to hide from the police. But this could get terribly involved. Please be reasonable. Two thousand."

He could hardly imagine what the crate must contain if the receipt for it was worth two thousand. He would drop by the warehouse and see if there was a way to peek inside. Then, if it was only a painting, nothing sinister or illegal, he would deliver the receipt for free. Meantime, Eileen and her playmate could sweat.

"I might go along at two thousand," he said. "I'll think it over and we'll discuss it again."

"Come over here now. I'll have the money ready."

"Where are you?"

"Same place—14A."

"Mr. Kavanagh's apartment?"

There was a silence.

"Are you on?" he said.

"Yes. Mr. Kavanagh's apartment. He's a very good friend."

"He'd have to be."

"Are you coming over?"

"I can't."

"Why not?" she nearly screamed.

"I have something to do. A business appointment. I could make it at…" He studied his watch. "At three this afternoon."

"Please don't be late, then. I'll expect you promptly at three. And I'll have the money."

"Sure you will. And maybe a little bonus. We'll discuss it."

He hung up, grinning broadly. She deserved his little revenge. He only wished there was within him just a bit more larceny. Then he would accept the two thousand. Perhaps, in spite of a stupidly conventional conscience, he could talk himself into it. Because God Almighty, how he needed that money!

Much would depend on what he found in the crate.

CHAPTER 7

He walked uptown, then west to the warehouse of the storage company. He could have two thousand by mid-afternoon—just for the asking. If Eileen Taggart had that kind of money she'd never miss it. And he was a fool, like all the slaves in a million offices who couldn't grab an opportunity if it had the least smell of evil.

It was a squat, sooty-gray building near the river. He pulled at a heavy door and passed inside. There was a long counter, behind which clerks and typists huddled over their desks. A bulky man with a meaty face and steel-rimmed glasses appeared.

"What can I do for you, sir?"

Norris produced the slip and handed it over. "I'd like to take a look at this shipment," he said. "There may be some things I want to leave in storage."

Somehow he expected the clerk to scrutinize him closely, asking sharp questions with an air of suspicion. On the contrary, the man hardly gave him a glance. He studied the slip, scratching his belly, yawning, and then he went off without a word.

The clerk returned in a minute, shaking his head. "No, sir," he said. "Can't see this one. Not today. Hasn't arrived yet. It's still in transit from Miami. You could try late tomorrow afternoon, Friday for sure. Better yet, you give us a call. Save you a trip. When you phone, give the clerk this invoice number in the right-hand corner. Okay?"

"Thanks," said Norris, taking back the receipt. "I'll remember."

He turned away quickly and went out.

He was vastly disappointed. He could stall for time, of course, but he was sick of the whole business. Better to spend his energy looking for work. He could ask the police to step in and take over. But on what grounds? He could imagine the questions and complications which would follow. No, he'd give the receipt to Eileen Taggart, and be done with it. If she was willing to pay two thousand bucks, the crate was loaded with trouble. He didn't want to get involved, but without searching for it, trouble found him easily enough.

Having a little extra time, he went up to his room and got out the correspondence in answer to his job applications. He made several calls, but was unable to make a single appointment.

At twenty-five minutes before three, he left the room, locking the door behind him. He went down the hall and pressed the button at the elevator. Waiting, he lit a cigarette. In a moment, he heard mounting steps, and two men—tall, crew-cut blondes with massive builds and alien faces—came onto the floor from a stairway. He recognized them instantly. He stood rooted by the elevator, watching.

He was not at all surprised to see them pause in their furtive hunting along the corridor at his own door. As one of them knocked, he swung towards Norris at the elevator. On his face there was not a flicker of recognition or interest. At first the knocking was soft, a secret sound, full of implication, then loud and staccato.

The men looked at each other and one of them began to reach into his pocket. Not for a gun, Norris was sure, but for some clever bit of metal to open a door.

Then the elevator came. And in heart-thumbing sweat, Norris got on and descended. At that moment he would gladly have paid Eileen Taggart to take the receipt off his hands.

Norris did not see Henry at the apartment building on Fifth Avenue. According to the boy who took him up to fourteen, Henry began his night duty at seven.

Standing before the door to 14A, Norris glanced nervously at his watch. It was two minutes after three. In another minute Eileen Taggart would have the receipt and in five, he would be gone. He would take no money. There would be no silly revenge, no more weird little games. For him it was over. When strange characters begin to hunt you down with God knows what intent, even if they find what they are looking for, it was time to make a fast exit. He would send someone for his bag and he would get lost somewhere in the city or on the island. Even so, it might be weeks before he stopped peering over his shoulder.

He pressed the button. A chime echoed solemnly. He waited, listening for her step. He heard nothing and in a moment rang again.

He tried the door. It was locked. He jabbed the button furiously, heard the chime echoes collide in a frantic dissonance. In the aftermath he heard light quick steps muted by carpeting. Then nothing, though he knew someone listened behind the door with a tension he could almost feel.

He knocked loudly. "C'mon, c'mon!" he called. "It's Paul Norris."

The door opened.

She was not so tall as Eileen Taggart. Nor as flamboyant. But perhaps a year or two younger. She had blue-black hair arranged in a short pageboy. And lavender eyes which were both wide and elliptical. Her features were delicate, barely accented by makeup, except for the rich mouth, florid in contrast to a skin gone pale with shock.

Yes, he could see in her eyes the fear which had drained color from her face. Her features were pulled tight with the effort for composure.

He glanced at the door. It was 14A all right.

"Who are *you?*" he said.

"Are you looking for Mr. Kavanagh? I'm Marian Collison, his personal secretary."

"I don't even know Mr. Kavanagh," he answered, studying her. She wore a tailored, charcoal-gray suit which might have been too severe on anyone with a lesser figure. She was utterly feminine. "I came to see Eileen Taggart," he added. "She was expecting me at three. I'm Paul Norris."

"Sorry," she said abruptly. "You must have the wrong apartment."

She kept the door partly closed, holding it for support, sagging against the jamb.

"You all right?" he asked. "You look sick."

"Please go now," she said. "I'm very busy."

She began to close the door but he made a wedge with his foot. There was something wrong. She was lying about Eileen Taggart, and he was not going to be left with that receipt.

"If you don't leave," she said, "I'll call the police."

"And if you don't let me see Eileen Taggart, I'll call them for you." He pushed past her into the living room.

For a moment, they stood staring at each other. Then she closed the door and slumped against it. Trance-like, her lower lip trembling, she gestured weakly.

"In there," she murmured.

He went quickly, pausing in the bedroom doorway.

She lay obliquely across the bed, her arms flung back, hands dangling over the side. Her dress had been torn upward from the skirt. She was naked from the waist down. Ripped panties and a garter belt dangled from her right ankle, the spiked shoes were twisted oddly on her narrow feet.

Norris recoiled, then moved into the room and stood over her.

The face was puffed and brutally beaten, the skin blue with purple tones. A coiled snake of leather, still around the neck, had strangled her. Eileen Taggart's tongue lolled. One eye was staringly open, the other closed, as if obscenely arranged.

Her pocketbook was on the floor. He picked it up absently. The purse contained nothing but keys, cosmetics and a torn envelope bearing his name. Mechanically he stuffed the envelope into his pocket, dropped the purse and fled from the room.

Marian Collison came from behind the bar with a glass in her hand. "You'll need a drink," she said, and he took the glass, gulping down the amber fire with the same absentness.

They fell into chairs.

"I hope," said Miss Collison, after a long moment," you weren't close." Her voice sounded pale and far away.

"No," he said. "I met her yesterday for the first time."

"Horrible," said Miss Collison brokenly. "Raped," she whispered.

Norris dipped his head. "Probably. But it must have been an afterthought." He reached in his pocket and found the receipt, holding it aloft. "She was murdered for this."

Marian Collison struggled to her feet and took the paper from his hand. She examined it carefully.

"Yes," she said. "For this. I'm sure you're right."

"You know what it is?" He glanced up at her.

She frowned, chewed her lip. "Not entirely. I know that the crate is holding something worth millions. And that it was stolen from Mr. Kavanagh."

"What?" he said, still in the fog of shock. "Millions!"

"Millions." She handed him the paper, and at the same time something changed in her face. The flaccid quality was gone. Her eyes squinted with determination.

"Mr. Ferris," she said.

"Norris."

"All right, Norris. We can't lounge about here in a stupor. Something's got to be done." She walked away, turned. "Are you ready to get involved in this thing? With the police and all the questions? And the headlines?"

"Not if I can help it. Publicity is just what I don't need." He thought of the two blonde men at the door to his room. Of course, they had beaten his name and his hotel out of Eileen Taggart, before they killed her. "No," he said. "I don't want to be involved."

"Neither do I," she cried. "I just got here. About five minutes ago. Mr. Kavanagh wanted me to stock the apartment with food, see that everything was in order. And—and then I found that. Oh God. Oh, my God. No! No, I mustn't let go. Mr. Kavanagh needs me. He'll want to handle this with the police in his own way, so there won't be any foul implications. I've been trying to reach him. I'll call again now. But are you willing to cooperate, Mr. Norris?"

"How?"

"Just say nothing until we can discuss it with Mr. Kavanagh."

"All right, That's reasonable. Anyway, I have nothing to do with this. I'm a complete outsider. Eileen Taggart picked me up when I got off the plane from Miami. Before that I never heard of her."

"How did you get that receipt then?" asked Miss Collison.

He told her the story, racing over the details.

"All right," she said. "I see exactly how it happeed. Mr. Kavanagh is going to be extremely grateful for that receipt. I just can't tell you. Now I'll call him again. And then we'll go over to his office and let him make the decisions. His days are full of decisions. He'll know what to do," she said proudly.

CHAPTER 8

They came out into the sunlight of Fifth Avenue. It was a warm day, and Norris had not brought his polo coat. Marian Collison shaded her eyes, searching for a cab. Impatience was described on her face, nothing else. She had not once mentioned the horror in the bedroom of 14A since talking with Mr. Kavanagh on the telephone. Her concentration seemed elsewhere. Norris observed that the ability to turn one's attention from immediate tragedy to expedient details was a gift—or a lack of imagination. In either case, he admired Miss Collison with her quick mentality. You would be able to count on her in almost any situation. And she was nice to look at. Very.

"You'd think it was raining," he said. "Not an empty cab in sight." Better to follow her lead and give the impression that nothing was on the mind but casual interests. The doorman was listening. He had greeted Miss Collison by name and must have remembered Norris entering the building twenty minutes before.

"I think," said Miss Collison, "it would be best for us to start walking downtown. We might find a cab at one of the cross streets. Please, Mr. Norris, let's hurry."

He fell in beside her and they moved off.

"If there's anything I detest," she said, "it's to stand around like an idiot when there are things to be done. If only you didn't always have to depend on other people. Even to get from one place to another." There wasn't the faintest suggestion of trouble in her voice. A marvelous actress—or was she?

"How far do we have to go?" he said.

"Down to thirty-seventh. The Empire State Building. And then straight up, seventy-one stories."

Approaching the corner, Norris looked back. One of the two brush-haired blondes with the Nordic features, (they seemed nearly alike), was paying off a cab. The other was talking to the doorman who was pointing in their direction.

Norris caught her arm. "Listen to me and don't argue," he hissed. "Those foreign looking bastards are talking to the doorman. They're about to come after us. Just stand here a moment, don't turn your head. But when I give the signal, run east, around the corner. When we're out of sight, I'll pass you the receipt. Then duck into a doorway, and I'll lead them off in another direction."

She got the drift immediately.

"Right," she said, making her face smiling and innocuous, her eyes on his. "Meet me at the Empire. In the lobby."

Norris had his hand on the paper in his pocket. He had changed his position enough so that he could see back over her shoulder. The two had finished with the doorman. They were moving down the block at an unhurried pace, trying to pretend indifference with set faces. Norris estimated a half block advantage.

"Go!" he said.

She bolted around the corner. Then he caught her and pushed the paper into her outstretched hand. She continued another twenty feet to the doorway of an apartment house. Then she vanished inside and for seconds he was on the street alone, but for cars and a woman wheeling a carriage in the other direction. Marian Collison would be all right. She would get lost in that building. Now he was on his own.

He was dashing across the street when they rounded the corner in full stride, leaping towards him with such easy power that he knew it was going to take more than speed.

Missing the girl, they broke stride. One shouted something at the other. A terse command, a harsh garbled sound. It wasn't English. Then they hammered after him at an intercepting diagonal, for he had crossed over and was sprinting back towards Fifth and those crowded walks where he might even get help.

It was too late to reverse direction, anyhow. They had separated in order to box him either way. He could only go on to the one who had gained the walk just in front of him and was setting himself squarely.

Norris did not falter as was expected of him. In the last moment he increased his speed and hurled himself at the man, sidestepping at the instant before impact, ramming a fist obliquely at the jaw, connecting, passing on.

It never occurred to him that such a thing could happen in broad daylight. But it did. Behind him a shot lashed the air. He heard the whip-snap of the slug first, saw a man just entering the block grab his shoulder, the most unbelieving expression on his face, and sink to his knees.

They were coming on behind him again, the lead blonde shoving a Luger into his pocket. A small crowd had gathered around the wounded man. No one helped him. Others watched the chase with dumb curiosity, yet not a person moved to interfere, nor even to summon the police. This was New York.

Then Norris saw the bus. A double-decker with the open stairway. The bus was already in motion, but traffic held its progress to a crawl. Amidst a cacophony of horn and brake sounds, he raced across the avenue. His hand reached out for the rail. His fingers nearly touched it as he ran. But then the bus accelerated and left him in a burst of speed.

Now he was on the opposite sidewalk, still running. He was drained. He was giving out fast. His throat felt seared with each raw gasp for air. And a pivot of his head had told him they were fifty yards behind.

All the people on the walk ahead seemed absurdly aimless. They shuffled along as if nothing had ever happened to them, or ever would. Their pallid faces turned at the sound of his pounding feet, a bit quizzical, but oddly lifeless. In his desperation, their bovine unconcern angered him.

Perhaps it was just that very remote edge of bitterness which made him do it—made him grab the door handle of the nearest car halted at the stoplight. Grabbing it, he pushed the button, swung the door and leaped in beside the astonished driver, a gray little man with a pinched face under a dark homburg.

"Drive!" he barked, shoving a knuckle of the hand in his pocket against the man's ribs. "Drive, you sonofabitch! Or I'll blow you to hell!"

"I can't," the man whimpered. "The light, the light!"

"Never mind the light!"

But fortunately the signal just then flicked green and the car crouched and spun ahead.

CHAPTER 9

"So what finally happened?" said Miss Collison as they hurried through the Empire State lobby toward the elevator.

"Oh, I goosed the old guy around a few corners and made him let me out at a subway. He was never so glad to get rid of anyone in his life."

"Fast thinking," she said, "from the very beginning. You're good in a tight spot. And you probably saved my life." She handed him the receipt for the crate. "I think you should give this to Mr. Kavanagh yourself," she said. "It'll make an impression."

"Why should I want to impress Mr. Kavanagh?"

They reached a waiting elevator and stepped in.

"Because someday he might do you some good. He never forgets a friend—or an enemy."

The elevator rose. It whispered aloft in a hollow sigh of air. The two were silent in the hem of people. Norris watched the wink of floor lights. He was tense and excited. But no longer frightened. You met a challenge only because you had to, and then suddenly you felt equal to anything.

The elevator paused and they alighted.

"Seventy-one," he said. "Home of the high and the mighty."

She gave him a look which was mildly amused and at the same time rebuking. He followed her around a bend to double doors of opaque glass. A gold script spoke modestly of the Kavanagh Holding Company.

They went in.

At the end of the corridor, Miss Collison opened a door marked E. T. Kavanagh, President. A girl transcribed shorthand into typed meaningful phrases. She looked up.

"He's waiting for you, Miss Collison. Impatiently, I might add."

Marian Collison raised an eyebrow, said, "Have a seat, Mr. Norris."

She slipped behind a heavy door. Norris could imagine a door of such thickness withholding secrets from the sharpest ears. He sat down with a magazine. He chose an article and read the first page. The door opened again. Miss Collison beckoned. He went in.

Everett Kavanagh was something of a surprise. He was not at all imposing in the classic sense. A rather small man approaching fifty, of almost delicate frame and feature. He had heavy brows and black hair. His nose was small and sharp, his thin lips hinted an ascetic nature.

He stood slowly behind the desk, his long pale fingers pressing polished tips to the surface. Slowly, too, he extended a hand, and Norris grasped it mechanically, caught by the eyes. Dark brown eyes in deep sockets, calm as mountain lakes in winter, with their surface gleam and shadow.

The hand was dry and bone-hard. It fell away and Mr. Kavanagh said, "I don't imagine you'll forget a day like this one, Mr. Norris." He spoke softly in measured tones. His lips played with a smile. He sat down, as did Norris and Miss Collison.

"I won't forget," said Norris. "There are people who may not let me."

Mr. Kavanagh toyed with a red and gold pen. Over his shoulder a gray-white tendril of cloud smoked the sky.

"We're everlastingly grateful to you, Mr. Norris," he said. "I have the story from Miss Collison." His lips twisted with displeasure, nostrils dilated. "Sordid, unthinkably brutal. I'm waiting now for a call from the police. She was a friend of mine. I don't know how this will be handled. But it must be done with discretion. In my position it would be a crushing scandal. You understand?"

"I think so. I don't envy you."

"It would be less ironic if I knew the girl. But I didn't. Not really."

"You didn't? Well, I thought—"

"She was the girl friend of Mr. Kavanagh's manager"—interrupted Miss Collison—"Harry Wheeler. He took care of the Miami house and certain business matters for Mr. Kavanagh, especially in Mr. Kavanagh's absence. When you mentioned Wheeler, I couldn't take time to explain."

"Wheeler had the key to my apartment," Kavanagh said. "I trusted him without reservation. A great mistake. I met Eileen Taggart just once. Socially I had nothing to do with her. Yet, will anyone believe it? With that girl dead in my apartment? So you see, the whole dirty business has got to be kept from the newspapers until her killer is found. But never mind, that's my problem."

He paused, swung to the window and back.

"Now, in spite of the fact that a human life has been taken, the crate, this property which has been stolen from me, is more important. We can't bring Eileen Taggart to life, but we can probably recover the very thing which killed her. Of course greed really destroyed her, but in a sense… Do you have the receipt, Mr. Norris?"

"Right here, sir." He passed the paper across the desk and Mr. Kavanagh bent over it.

"How simple," he said. "And yet effective." He spoke to Miss Collison. "Who would ever guess that anything so valuable would be shipped on a van as household goods?"

Miss Collison nodded her agreement.

"And then they had the gall to use my apartment as a hideout."

"Clever," said Miss Collison. "Because no one would ever expect to find them there."

"I suppose they planned to change their names," said Mr. Kavanagh.

"Naturally," said Miss Collison.

"And then leave the country with false papers."

"Probably," said Miss Collison.

"I'm more than curious," said Norris. "Would you mind telling me, sir, what's in the crate that's so valuable?"

"I can certainly understand your curiosity," said Mr. Kavanagh patiently. "And I'd like very much to indulge it, especially since we owe you so much more than a mere explanation, but I'm afraid I can tell you nothing. Not at this time. Perhaps never."

"Never?"

Mr. Kavanagh sighed. He studied the red and gold pen. "You see," he said, "although the contents of the crate belong to me exclusively, they are secret. How shall I explain? Well, let me put it this way. The whole business has a certain national significance, even international. If the information should leak further, there would be a mad race for possession and more bloodshed. And if this thing got into the wrong hands, our country would be undermined. It would be extremely dangerous. Therefore, it would be most ill-advised for me to trust a single person. Even Miss Collison, whose loyalty is beyond question, had been kept in the dark."

"What about Wheeler?" said Norris, who was more confused than ever. "How did he know?"

"Oh, he didn't," said Mr. Kavanagh. "He merely suspected. He saw the possibility for a huge personal profit. He had a little knowledge. He knew that something of enormous value was being shipped to me from abroad. He knew only the approximate date of delivery. I didn't know precisely myself. It could have been three or four weeks, one way or another."

Mr. Kavanagh lighted a cigarette and puffed thoughtfully.

"Since I didn't have the exact date of delivery," he went on, "and since I could not get a promise of that date, I didn't feel that I could sit around idly waiting. There were important clients to deal with. They came to Miami, and I took them on my yacht for a cruise around the Bahamas. It may sound casual, but much business is done that way. Meanwhile, Wheeler was to notify me of the shipment. We were in touch. I was to fly back immediately.

"But what happened? While I was gone the delivery was made. Wheeler said nothing. Instead he played my part. He passed himself off as Everett Kavanagh. It was easy because he was in my house. And the men who delivered the box had never met me. They were little more than carriers. Agents, you might say. And the servants were under Wheeler's control. He had dismissed them for the day.

"There was one hitch. A large sum of money was to be paid for the shipment. By this time Wheeler knew how much and what for. He had talked with one of the agents the day before delivery. So he pretended to have the money. He lured the men into the house with the box. They were armed. Even so, as per agreement, they searched him. Then they opened the box for his inspection. Whereupon, Eileen Taggart stepped out of hiding with a repeating shotgun. The men were locked in a storeroom and Wheeler and Taggart fled with the shipment. One of the servants returned unexpectedly, heard shouts and pounding, let the men out. The servant phoned Miss Collison and she got hold of me. But by then, it was too late."

"My God," said Norris. "What did you do, call the police?"

"No," replied Kavanagh. "Calling the police meant explanations. You don't tell police to run around hunting for a stolen box. They want to know what's in the box. And I'm pledged to secrecy. No, I got in touch with someone in Washington, and I put some private operatives on the job. But nothing turned up until now, thanks to you, sir."

"Well," said Norris, "since you didn't pay for the box, why did you bother tracing it?"

"Because I assume full responsibility for its loss. And because I absolutely must find it, take possession and pay over the money. The contents of the box are all-important to me. Comparatively, the money is so much paper."

"I have a confession to make," said Norris. "I went over to Morgan's warehouse and inquired about the crate. It hasn't arrived. It's still in transit."

Mr. Kavanagh smiled benignly. "I like your honesty, Norris. But I'm already aware that the crate has not arrived. Miss Collison has a photographic memory. After you showed her the receipt, she gave me all the information on the phone, including the invoice number. I called Morgan Van Lines in Florida. The crate has not arrived, true. In fact it never left Miami. Not for New York. Wheeler caught it just in time. He was remembered by the clerk, showed identification anyway, and had the crate sent elsewhere."

"Good God! Where?" said Norris.

"To San Diego, and," said Kavanagh solemnly, "that's right across the border from Mexico."

CHAPTER 10

Mr. Kavanagh stared below at the city. Norris and Miss Collison exchanged glances.

"It would seem to me," said Norris, "that you could establish your right to the crate and have it picked up in San Diego."

Mr. Kavanagh returned his attention slowly, as if from some distant speculation.

"He's right," said Miss Collison. "I hardly think the Morgan Van Lines would argue with someone in your position, sir."

"I wish I could make you people underatand how impossible it is to deal with this situation in terms of simple, direct action." Mr. Kavanagh spoke indulgently, as if to children. "In this case, every normal procedure is closed to me. Naturally, I could claim what's mine, prove theft and take possession. But again, that would mean disclosing the contents of the crate. Don't you see?"

Norris and Miss Collison lapsed into silence. You couldn't argue with the unknown.

"No," said Mr. Kavanagh, "unfortunately I'm compelled to be just as sneaky, just as sly as Wheeler." He chuckled mirthlessly. "In a sense, I'm going to have to steal back what has been taken from me and the agents who delivered it. But we'll come to that. Now, Mr. Norris, I want to do something for you, and I hope that you won't misunderstand. I want to offer you a position with the Kavanagh Company. And I assure you that my motive in doing so is not pure gratitude. I think you are a man of integrity. You might have attempted to steal the crate for yourself. At the very least, you could have held me up for plenty. You did neither. You handled yourself with intelligence and imagination, and also, bravery. You certainly saved Miss Collison's life."

Norris tried to look casual. He said nothing.

"Would you like to work for me, Mr. Norris?"

"I don't know," replied Norris honestly. "I appreciate the offer. But I don't see how I would fit. I know as much about a holding company as I do astronomy. I could point out the north star and the big dipper on a clear night. And that's it."

"Let me tell you something," said Mr. Kavanagh, leaning forward, speaking earnestly. "I don't buy a man's precise knowledge of facts and figures in my line. I don't buy his past experience in my business. I buy qualities, Mr. Norris. I buy honesty. I buy intelligence, basic intelligence. I buy energy. I buy courage and imagination. These are the things I pay for, Mr. Norris. With such qualities I can teach a man anything!"

"I suppose that's true," said Norris. "And I'm flattered. But I wonder, sir, if you're not overrating me on the basis of one incident. I've had some failures which might pop up to accuse me later. Actually, you know nothing at all about me."

Mr. Kavanagh leaned back and expelled a jet of smoke ceilingward. He appeared to be secretly amused. His head came down abruptly and his eyes were almost frighteningly intense.

"Do you think," he said, "that I operate a business of this stature willy-nilly? Hit or miss? Of course I know all about you." He leaned back again and addressed the ceiling.

"Let's see. Paul Norris, Age, thirty-four. In September of this year. Residence, Miami, Florida. Until yesterday when you took a room at a hotel in this city. You were employed for five years and eight months by Hoffman, Lewis and Pearson, advertising. Account executive, the Miami office. Salary—one hundred and seventy-five dollars weekly. You were progressive and reliable, the quality of your work was excellent. Until your wife, a real estate agent, became enamored of a builder, Herbert Worley. And divorced you to marry the same. From the time your wife announced the decision, you began to drink. You went on intermittent binges. Your work fell off. You came to the office late, frequently you were absent. You were fired. At least you were put on notice. You came to New York seeking a similar placement with the home office. You failed to secure the position because of office politics. You are presently unemployed." Kavanagh leaned forward again. "And, mister, you need a job! Do you want it?"

"God Almighty!" Norris exploded. "How did you—"

"I have my ways," said Kavanagh mysteriously. "And a man should be forgiven a justifiable mistake. Do you want to work for me, Norris?"

"Well, sure," said Norris. "And thanks. But on what terms?"

"Two hundred a week, and you'll earn it!"

"I expect to. In what department?"

"We'll see. There's advertising here, of course. Right now you'll report directly to me. And your first assignment will be to grab the six-twenty-five jet flight to Los Angeles. Proceed from there to San Diego. Take this receipt and bring back that crate! Miss Collison will accompany you."

Norris was astonished. Reluctantly he took the invoice from Mr. Kavangh's outstretched hand.

"I realize," said Kavanagh, watching him closely, "that this is an unusual request. But that shipment, however secret, was company business, and I want a company representative to handle the recovery. In the event that the matter becomes exposed to the police, it would give our actions a certain legality. But I have much more valid reason for sending you, in particular, Norris. Outside of Wheeler, the agents involved and myself, there are only two other people who have even a superficial knowledge of the value of that crate. You're one. Miss Collison is the other. Obviously, if I turn the matter over to still another person, the risk of a leak becomes greater. The secret must be kept among us. You understand?"

"Yes, sir. But what about the private operatives you mentioned? I assume you mean detectives. Don't they know anything?"

"No. They were to locate Wheeler and Eileen Taggart and report to me, nothing else."

"Is it possible then," said Norris, "that those were the men who tried to grab Wheeler at the terminal in Miami?"

"Again, no. My men could not find a trace of Wheeler or Taggart. But we haven't time for further questions." Kavanagh looked at his watch. "Are you willing to make the trip to San Diego?"

"Do I have a choice?"

Mr. Kavanagh smiled. "I grant you there are risks. If you're afraid—"

"Of course I'm afraid." Norris glanced at Miss Collison. "I'm not stone."

"Good," said Kavanagh. "A man who is decently afraid will be careful."

"If there might be trouble," said Norris, "why send Miss Collison?"

"For that very reason. If there is trouble of any sort, Miss Collison will contact me immediately. Meanwhile, she'll stay in the background."

"In other words, if she doesn't hear from me—"

"Exactly."

"My God!"

"Don't be alarmed, Norris. I don't think you have anyone to fear presently but Wheeler. And I'll have him picked up before he ever gets to the Morgan warehouse in San Diego."

"I feel as if I've just been signed by the FBI," said Norris.

"There is a similarity," granted Kavanagh with a wry smile. "Except that after this little errand you return to normalcy. Now—for the details. Miss Pelham, she's the girl outside my office, will have two prepaid reservations on the six-twenty-five jet to Los Angeles. Allowing for the three-hour differential, you'll arrive at five minutes past eleven, Pacific Coast time. You'll be met at the terminal by a man named Garvin. Now this Garvin is a chauffeur, a kind of factotum to a friend of mine—Gus Dasher. Mr. Dasher has a lovely little house on the coast at La Jolla. And Dasher will put you up at his place during your stay. He's under obligation for many reasons. But he's gracious and he'll be glad to do it anyway. La Jolla is a charming town and it's almost on top of San Diego. Norris can commute as necessary. Miss Collison will not leave the house, but will keep in touch with me by phone. Garvin will take you there directly from the plane and all in all it will be most convenient. Clear so far?"

"Clear enough," said Norris, "except that I'm out of breath just listening." He looked to Miss Collison, who merely shrugged as if this sort of breakneck organizing had long ago become routine.

"There are times when you have to make quick decisions," said Kavanagh, "and gamble a little that you've chosen the right people to carry them out."

"True," said Norris. "But in such a short time, how could you—"

"Mr. Bell solved many problems, my friend. There's hardly anything that can't be accomplished in five minutes by this simple act." Kavanagh lifted the receiver from the phone, gently replaced it. "But please, let me finish.

"The crate will be traveling by van and these vans are not exactly famous for speed. I imagine you'll arrive three or four days too early, not forgetting that these big trucks haul around the clock. So I'd like you to use the extra time well, Mr. Norris. For instance, you could ingratiate yourself with just the right clerk at Morgan's warehouse. A twenty dollar bill often produces cooperation. More gives the impression of a bribe. A bribe is suspicious and therefore dangerous." Kavanagh stood and began to pace slowly. "You must, of course, get exactly the right man at the warehouse, or the effort is wasted. Then you give him an acceptable story—something about various items like cooking utensils, dishes and so on, without which you and your wife cannot set up housekeeping. And you would be much obliged if the clerk would call you immediately upon the arrival of the shipment. If at that point he takes the twenty, you're set.

"Meanwhile, you rent a pickup truck so as to be ready to personally take delivery. The next step is going to take still more thought and planning. I'll have to make an arrangement. But I can give you instructions on the phone long before. And finally, remember that Dasher knows only that you are attending to some routine business for me and he is to be kept in complete ignorance of the truth."

Kavanagh paused in stride, rubbed his nose with a forefinger. "Let's see, now. Yes, one more thing. Miss Pelham will have two weeks advance pay for both of you, plus five hundred dollars expense money, all cash. You will sign for the money; and, Mr. Norris, be good enough to leave your social security number and tax information with Miss Pelham. By this time your name has already been added to the payroll."

"I'll be damned!" said Norris. "How could you be so sure of me?"

"Don't forget that you're now an employee," said Mr. Kavanagh sternly. But then he smiled. "You see," he said, "I was prepared to make it worth your while, one way or another. Just a bit more resistance and your salary might have gone up considerably. No, don't be disappointed. If you're successful there will be a handsome bonus."

He winked broadly at Miss Collison, extended his hand to Norris. "And now goodbye. Take a cab to the airport. And I wish you luck. You may need it."

CHAPTER 11

Evening along the Grand Central Parkway. The driver remembered his lights and reached for the switch. The cab scurried through traffic towards Idlewild. Norris had checked out of the hotel in a wild scramble, harried still more by the discovery that his room had been searched. His bag rested in the trunk beside Miss Collison's overnight case. He sighed.

"Again," he said.

"Again what?" Miss Collison returned.

"Idlewild. Another plane. It's a treadmill. I have this feeling that it won't stop, either. I fell out of the sky yesterday, and today I'm gone again. I remember my name but I don't know where I live. Do you?"

"La Jolla. Someplace in La Jolla. Care of Gus Dasher."

"Fine. Nice orientation. Thanks. No, really. It's been a nightmare. I can't adjust. I try, but I don't feel as if I belong. Not even to the Kavanagh Company."

Miss Collison smiled and gave his hand a quick pat. "You'll get over it," she said. "Or you'll get used to it. I have."

"You travel a lot, Miss Collison? Listen, do we have to keep up the formality? For three days, a week? I'm Paul and it's Marian, isn't it?"

"Marian. Yes, I do travel quite a bit: between New York and Miami; anyplace Mr. Kavanagh sends me."

"How do you like working for him?"

"I find it stimulating. Mr. Kavanagh has a mind like one of those giant computers: steel-hard, fast and precise. You can't keep up with him. It's tiring. But also challenging."

Marian Collison opened her purse and removed a large combination case and lighter. The gadget looked too big for small, dainty hands. She had changed from the austere suit into a burnt orange dress. It was a happy transformation. She had a charming figure, artfully assembled. Away from the brisk Kavanagh environment she seemed to gather her own personality. It was less brittle, more feminine. There was warmth to her. It came out in unexpected moments. Yet Norris decided that she would not be easy to know in any total sense. There was something abstract in her mentality. He couldn't reach it.

He took the cigarette she offered from the ebony square of a case and she flared the lighter.

"Do you always stay at the Waldorf, Marian?" She had stopped there to change and pick up her overnight bag. He was a little surprised. He had thought perhaps she might be a Kavanagh fixture in 14A over on Fifth.

"Oh, yes. When I'm in town. And when Mr. Kavanagh is paying the tab. I have an apartment in Miami."

"Married?"

"No."

"Ever?"

"My husband was killed in an accident."

"Oh? Sorry."

She didn't explain, and intuition told him to drop the subject.

"I'm glad for you," she said. "About the job." She sat serenely in her corner, jogging with the motion of the cab. She seemed perfectly poised. But in the spaced glare of headlights her eyes were troubled.

"Thanks," he said. "I should be happy. I should damn well be elated. But I'm not."

"Depressed?"

"Very."

"So am I."

"Eileen Taggart?"

She nodded. "As long as I live, I'll never forget the way she looked. I couldn't help thinking how frail we are. How vulnerable, and temporary. Suddenly I had the urge to pounce on life. Devour it. Live furiously. And I hated myself. For being typically selfish. Not wanting to see anyone so shockingly, so convincingly dead. Because someday the same filthy pointless joke is going to be played on me, too."

"That sounds pretty grim. You trying to say that you're living as dangerously as Eileen Taggart was?"

"No, I didn't mean that at all."

But he wasn't so sure.

"Let's forget it," she said.

"Sure. Why should we be morbid? We're on a kind of paid vacation."

She gave him a long look. "I wouldn't be too sure. Mr. Kavanagh could make a trip to the moon sound simple and orderly, but after you leave him you realize that he didn't mention how you get back."

"With a box of goodies worth millions," said Norris. "Aw, come on now. Millions?"

"That's what he told me, and he wasn't smiling."

"Taggart said the box would contain a valuable painting surrounded by household knick-knacks."

"That's ridiculous!" Marian snorted.

"Then you do know what it is."

"Even if I did, I couldn't tell you. Anyway, have you ever heard of a single painting worth millions? And what would a holding company want with it?"

"Well," he said, "I knew I was being snowed. I never seriously believed it was a painting. What's this Gus Dasher like?"

"I've never met him. You know as much about him as I do."

Norris puffed and was thoughtful. For a long space they were quiet. It was not an uncomfortable silence. He grew weary of probing for answers and made his mind a blank.

"There's Idlewild," said Marian. "I love flying. Do you?"

"Yes. But not in planes. I don't trust them."

"According to statistics—"

"I know," he finished, "more people die in the bathtub. And if you believe the advertising, these planes all crash in perfect safety. And comfort."

He squinted at his watch.

"How long?" she asked.

"Twenty-eight minutes."

"I wish it were five," said Marian.

"Why?"

"Because then we'd never make it."

CHAPTER 12

The plane was late. They could see no one in the L.A. terminal who might be Garvin, the chauffeur. Then mysteriously, just as they were claiming their luggage, the man appeared, as if he had been in the background all the time, mentally plucking them from the crowd; for he never seemed in any doubt.

"I'm Chuck Garvin," he said. "I'll take them bags. We got a pretty long pull, and Mr. Dasher, he's waitin' up."

Garvin was a long lanky type with a wise country-boy face. He had sunken cheeks and dark implacable eyes. His whole structure could be plainly traced. Where you couldn't see bone, you knew there was muscle. At one time or another his knobby hands were well acquainted with manual labor and Norris could picture him grasping and lifting under a raw sun with stoical deliberation.

He wore a visored cap but no uniform. Just a navy blue sport-shirt and slacks. His manner was taciturn, his servitude skin-deep and grudgingly accepted.

He picked up the bags and moved off with long strides, so that they had to push to keep up with him.

"How did you know us?" Norris asked.

"You can always tell," said Garvin, as if that was the complete answer. He didn't turn his head when he spoke. He kept shifting the gum in his mouth.

It was more than a car when they got to it. It was a black Cadillac limousine, hearse-like and just as long. Norris couldn't judge the year. Limousines had a way of looking alike. But it wasn't new for all its shine.

Garvin got the rear doors open and they climbed in, settled comfortably on the deep-cushioned expanse of seat as the chauffeur tossed the bags in the trunk and slid behind the wheel. Then they purred away into the night, soon picking up Sepulvida Boulevard, heading south.

The night was warm, the traffic thin. Garvin drove swiftly. The sleepy little towns along the highway, dots between dashes of open space, fell behind and were replaced by new ones. Only Long Beach with its endless clutter of squat buildings and pulsing traffic signals, delayed their progress. Then Seal Beach. And beyond it for miles, nothing but the dim wash of the Pacific, and sand. And across the highway, adding incongruity to the scene, a far reaching network of shadowy oil derricks. With pumps below their structures, steel arms rising and falling in perpetual rhythm.

Norris then said, "How would you like to own just one? I'd come down and park and watch the goddamn thing pump, and every time that baby gave a chug I'd say, there's five bucks, and five more, and another and another. What a beauty. It works while you sleep. It never stops. Barrels and barrels of slippery gold."

"Dream on," said Marian wearily.

"Tired? How do you feel?"

"Ask me in the morning," she said. "I could sleep."

"I hope Dasher won't expect us to make bright conversation into the wee hours."

She held a finger to her lips and nodded towards the ever-silent Garvin.

"Even when I get that oil well," said Norris softly, leaning close, "I won't have a chauffeur, or any kind of servant. No privacy. And secretly they hate you because you've got all that dough."

"Have you been out to the coast before, Paul?"

"Two or three times."

"So have I. But I don't know this section well. Do you?"

"Well enough."

"How far, then?" she said.

"Not much over an hour, I'd say. My God, this is crazy. Florida, New York and California. In only two days. Once in awhile I forget to think grimly and it's almost fun."

"Not for me," she said.

"You sound disenchanted."

"There's another word for it.

"Scared?"

"Yes. Aren't you?"

"Sometimes. Not at the moment."

"If you knew just a little more…. Anyway," she said, "as usual, ignorance is a kind of bliss."

He turned to look at her intently. "Care to explain that?"

"I really can't," she said. "But if you want to back out, I'll be the first to applaud you as a very smart guy. I could phone Mr. K. in the morning."

"You wouldn't think I was gutless?"

"Not at all."

"Well, I am. But I'm going on anyway. It's one of those compulsive tales. I've got to know the end."

"You want an end?" she said. "I'll give you an end. Eileen Taggart." She sighed and turned away to stare and stare out the window.

"Garvin," Norris raised his voice, "what does Mr. Dasher do for a living? We never met the gentleman."

"Sir?" Garvin turned his head in a way which suggested that he had not been listening at all, that he was far removed.

"I say, what sort of business is Mr. Dasher in?"

"He don't do much anymore," said Garvin. "Don't have to."

"Make his pile, did he?"

"His pile? Yeah, he made his pile. That's about it, sir."

Garvin returned his attention to the road, and Norris gave up. Let Dasher speak for himself.

In time they came to a fork. A road branched off to the right and Garvin swung onto it from the highway.

"La Jolla?" asked Marian.

"Think so," said Norris. "Daytime when I was here last. Just passing through at that. Garvin, is this the place?"

"Not far from here," he muttered.

They wound through dark and silent streets through a residential area of hovering palms and tidy lawns. The air was cool, tinged with flower scents, vaguely tropical, soporific. They moved seaward, then north along a cliff, turning suddenly into a driveway.

The place was not very large—a kind of oversized cottage, loosely Cape Cod design, white frame with green shutters and inset entranceway. The living room had a great bay window with small squares of glass. There were palms as always and a climb of bougainvillae above a two-car garage. A pale glow of light from the living room shadowed the lawn.

Norris had expected more, perhaps all Mr. Kavanagh's friends should be enormously wealthy.

Garvin went with them to the door, carrying the bags. He was lifting a hand to knock when the door opened. At the same moment a light flashed, revealing Mr. Gus Dasher.

Norris had thought Dasher would be older. Though he had perfectly white hair, he couldn't have been much beyond forty. A man just over middle height with a round face and extended ears. His lips were at once heavy and boyish, his chin sharp. He had very large, very round eyes which were pink lidded, and with his pale skin, he had the look of an albino.

"Come in, come in," he said. He spoke softly, as if there was a need for quiet. They followed him down two steps to a sunken oval living room, where he stood with his hand extended.

"Norris, of course, and Miss Collison. I've been waiting behind a book. Almost fell asleep." He wore maroon corduroy trousers and a gray shirt rolled above his biceps. "Glad you could come," he said. "A real pleasure. Garvin will take your bags to the spares and then we'll have a little drink, eh?"

Garvin took the cue and departed.

"Hell of an imposition," said Norris, "keeping you up half the night."

"Yes," said Marian. "You're very kind. Why don't you go off to bed and we'll see you in the morning?" She looked at her watch. "After all, it's—"

"I wouldn't hear of it. Got to have a nightcap with me anyway. For a good sleep, eh?" He still spoke softly, peering behind him down a narrow hallway. "Tell you what, though, if you don't mind, we'll go down to the playroom. Can't bother my kids, but the wife is a light sleeper."

"Sure thing," said Norris, who now understood Dasher's hushed manner.

They passed through the living room, with its maple pieces cheerfully upholstered, following Dasher into a kitchen of pale yellow. He opened a door and flicked the light switch.

"People don't go in for cellars much in this part of the country," said Dasher as they descended. "I have one of the few around. Got one room for the kids to go crazy in, another for the older lunatics."

It was a big square room of gray cement walls, one end of it wood-paneled behind a heavy oak bar. Great red leather chairs, a sofa, tables, lamps and throw rugs furnished the rest of it.

"How nice!" said Marian, seating herself beside Norris on the leather sofa. "Practical, too."

"Indestructible is the word," said Dasher from behind the bar. "What'll you folks have for a nightcap?"

"Scotch," said Marian. "And water."

"Bourbon," said Norris. "Just toss it over the rocks, if you will."

Dasher opened a small refrigerator and clunked ice into glasses. He lifted bottles from a wall cabinet and in a moment, served the drinks. He fell into a chair opposite and raised his glass. They drank.

"What brings you people to this part of the country?" inquired Dasher. His tone was casual, conversational.

"A business matter for Mr. Kavanagh," said Marian. "Mr. Norris and I will bring back some statistics on a San Diego firm which the company is investigating."

Mr. Dasher waited, looking mildly from one to the other.

When nothing further was forthcoming, he said, "Kavanagh is a brilliant man. A genius in his line."

"We like to think so," said Norris. He had decided that he would be businesslike.

"Yes," said Dasher. "I have the utmost respect for Everett. We've worked on several problems together and I've found him a shrewd businessman." He smiled, lifting his eyes which seemed to express the contemplation of handsome profits.

Norris felt the tension of the night recede, and he was growing relaxed. The pleasant room, the small talk, the charming company of Marian Collison, persuaded him that what had seemed a violent nightmare had become more a stimulating adventure. The affair of the invaluable box would be solved in good time. Anyway, there would be several days in which to luxuriate before the small risk. And then normalcy, with a bonus, approbation and enduring security. With Kavanagh behind him, he might rise to unlimited heights and big-money rewards. Yes, it was all paved road ahead and worth the detour. He was a mighty lucky guy.

"Do you have an office in San Diego, Mr. Dasher?" said Marian.

"No," he answered. "Not anymore."

"You can't be retired?" she came back.

"Not exactly. But I don't look for business. I'm on call for special assignments, you might say. When a man has enough, Miss Collison, he should learn to enjoy it. The accumulation of wealth beyond need is ridiculous, don't you think? A man who works for more than plenty has a disease." Mr. Dasher smiled indulgently. He brought a handkerchief from his pocket and, holding it to his nose, made a delicate sound.

"It's a disease I'm in no danger of catching," said Marian with a low chuckle.

Dasher's eyes gleamed with amusement.

"Nor I," said Norris. "What sort of business are you in, sir? I mean, when you work at it."

"Some people would call me an efficiency expert," said Dasher. "I don't like the term." He made a face of disgust. "I'm an organizer, a troubleshooter. When a business is failing, I hop in just at the edge of collapse and reorganize. I'm really an eraser on the blackboard of confusion." He smiled wryly, struck by the cleverness of his own explanation. "Yes, an eraser. I wipe out the old and make room for the new. I chop out the misfits—the unnecessary and the abortive workers. Though I deal with other facets, too, my specialty is personnel." He sat back a little smugly and made a pyramid of pale fingers.

At this point, Norris began to look upon Dasher with some dislike. Not an active dislike, since he could afford to be objective. Fatuous bastard, he thought. The great eraser. Ha!

"It sounds fascinating," he said, watching Marian from the corner of his eye. Her face was drawn in cordial lines, but her eyes were cool. "A big responsibility, Mr. Dasher. Playing god with so many people's lives. It must give you a magnificent feeling of power."

Marian sent him a darting look of caution and immediately he regretted the sarcasm. But it was lost upon Gus Dasher.

"No," he said. "Not especially. With me, the whole thing is completely impersonal. I have a job to do and I do it as precisely as a machine. How can it be otherwise? It's a poor simile, I know. But take, for instance, the executioner of cattle in a Chicago abattoir. Suppose the man wept every time he smashed the head of an animal? How efficient would that man be?"

"I see what you mean," said Marian without concealed repugnance.

"But let's not talk business," said Dasher. "I'm a terrible host. Won't you have something to eat after that long flight?"

"Please don't trouble," said Marian.

"Trouble? I press a button and Garvin does the rest. A sandwich? We have ham or cheese. How about turkey? Alice, my wife, is superb with a turkey."

"That sounds just right," said Marian. "Turkey."

"I prefer ham," said Norris. "If it's just as easy."

"Certainly," said Dasher. He stood and, reaching beneath the bar, pressed an invisible button. In seconds, there was the sound of feet on the stairs and Garvin appeared. Dasher gave him the order. "And don't be stingy," he added. "Dagwood had the right idea."

Garvin departed with a small bow.

They had barely begun a discussion of the corrosive effect of sea air on metal, the advantages and disadvantages of shore life over inland dwelling, when Garvin returned. He carried a small tray on which were two plates, each covered with an immaculate white napkin. He set the tray gently on a table beside Dasher.

"Well," said the latter heartily, "here we are!"

As Dasher reached for the napkin covering the nearest plate, Garvin stood by, apparently to see if anything further was needed. Dasher removed the napkin as if he were performing a trick, at least with the same gusto. There was a single, huge sandwich from which the crust had been neatly severed, with pickles, olives, and potato chips.

"Ah," said Dasher. "This must be the ham. Now, for the turkey."

He lifted the other napkin and there was the soft glint of blue steel.

Dasher plucked the .45 from the plate and aimed the barrel leisurely upon Norris and Marian Collison.

"Not exactly turkey," he said. "But a turkey-shooter, wouldn't you say, kids?"

CHAPTER 13

At first Norris thought it was a joke. Dasher was slightly amused, of course. But he wasn't joking.

"Norris," he said. "I want you to stand up and turn around. Marian, you stay right where you are like a good little girl. That's it."

"You won't find what you're looking for," said Norris. "I don't have the receipt with me." It was taped out of sight, inside the toe of his shoe.

"Receipt?" said Dasher. "What receipt? Is Kavanagh sending receipts for me to sign? That would be a new one. Just do as you're told—up and around!"

Norris obeyed. He heard a clatter of metal and Garvin approached behind him. His wrists were taken roughly and the cuffs clamped in place with a clicking sound. Searching hands swept over him for a weapon, but found nothing.

"Now you can turn and sit," said Dasher.

Hands locked behind him, Norris sat down awkwardly.

"Why don't you tell us what you want?" said Marian. She had gone exceedingly pale.

"Want?" said Dasher mildly. "I don't want anything. Did you think I was going to steal your money? Later, of course, since you won't need it.... But I'm well paid for this work, you know."

"What work?" said Norris.

"I told you before," answered Dasher impatiently. "You asked my business and I said, quite correctly, that I'm an eraser. I'm a troubleshooter; and I shoot trouble—with this." He waved the .45. "And you're in trouble. To Everett Kavanagh. He asked that you both be removed, and I'm most obliging, you see, at a price."

"Why?" cried Marian. "Why should he want us killed?"

"I don't know," said Dasher. He spoke sincerely. "I have no idea. Those things are never of interest to me. I have clients all over the country who send people to me. I never ask why. I ask, how much will you pay? That's what I ask. Some people come higher than others. It depends on their importance. And believe me, this is not an expensive job, as they go. You are not important. You'll hardly be missed."

He picked up the sandwich and bit carefully into it. For a moment he chewed. "Garvin," he said, and a piece of bread fell from mouth to lap, "go up and check the area. Then backup the station wagon and turn it around. Bring the tarp when you come down. The gentleman will go first. I'm in no hurry with the lady."

He gave Marian a lewd grin and took another bite of the sandwich.

"You know," he said moistly, his voice muffled with eating, "I used to be a mortician." He watched Garvin's retreating back. "And this is all duck soup to me. One body is like another. Receive and process. But since I got into the manufacturing end of the business, the money is so much better. Remarkable! A hit like this, ten thousand. One guy—he was a judge—got me twenty grand. Big man, big business for me, eh? So, all right. I was a mortician." He swallowed, took another bite. "I had a small funeral home. And I still own a piece of it. And then there's a crematorium. I own all of that now." He chewed thoughtfully. "You understand what a crematorium is? Sure you do. But I once knew a guy who thought they made cream in such a place. No, really! Now—a man's got access to a crematorium and that man is in the extermination business, but good. Right? Sure!

"You take the body and shove it into the furnace. Its flame takes a man's body and just gobbles it whole. Three, four hours later, what have you got? Nothing but a skeletal outline of bone ash. You could sweep it all into a shoe box and have space left over.

"Now I ask you, what kind of a story does a scattering of ashes in the wind have to tell? How clever can you get?"

He sighed and popped an olive into his mouth.

"I never go to a job. The action comes here. All of it. The suckers come on their feet and go out on their backs, into the station wagon, covered with a tarp, then down to the crematorium. Finished. I sit easy and wait for the next phone call, and a big envelope full of cash. Any questions?"

He smiled and shoved the last of the sandwich into his mouth.

"You filthy beast," said Marian. "Monster!"

"This guy is sick," Norris said. "But he understands money. And we could buy him off." He was thinking of the crate. Marian might know more than she admitted. Norris had not yet reached the raw end of his fear. It was all too fantastic to be true.

"You couldn't buy me with a million," said Dasher. "I make a contract and I keep it. I never cheat a client," he announced proudly.

"Listen," said Marian, straining forward. "You won't get away with it. There are people who would look for me, and never stop looking."

"Naturally," said Dasher, fingering the hammer of the automatic. "Of course they'll look for you. I'm always prepared for that. But where will they look? You think I give out this address? Did you ever know it? Or even a phone number? I have ways within ways. I have a hundred dodges. That's how I stay in business. But we'll talk later, you and I, of other things. Won't we? Sure we will. Right now, I think we should make Mr. Norris permanently comfortable."

Norris hear the hammer click, saw the round dark eye of the barrel center on his chest. He still couldn't quite believe it wasn't some play he watched from the first row.

"May I smoke?" said Marian with a tremulous voice. She opened her purse.

"No!" said Dasher. "Don't touch that pocketbook. Just toss it over here. That's it." He dumped the contents of the purse on the floor and slowly, watching them, put all it contained back inside. "Sometimes," he said, "little girls carry little guns. You can't be too careful." He tossed the purse. "Now you may smoke."

Marian brought out the ebony square of a cigarette case, the one which combined to make a lighter. Deliberately, she tapped a cigarette and Norris knew that, as before, she was merely stalling for time. Dasher watched her with half an eye as he adjusted the gun to aim again at Norris.

It happened then. The most unbelievable play of the night. Peering at Dasher with narrowed eyes, Marian brought the case up and thumbed the lighter. It fired. But oddly, the little flame came from the wrong end. And with it a thin sharp sound, like the snap of dry wood.

For a moment, Dasher seemed only startled. He flinched in his chair, his mouth fell open. He began to shift the gun towards Marian, who watched with the most intent expression Norris had ever seen. But Dasher was having trouble with the gun. It seemed too heavy in his hand. The hand dropped altogether. Then Dasher made a small gasp, and his head fell sideways.

Marian leaped up and crossed to bend over him. She turned. "Dead," she said.

"How?" said Norris in a voice stricken with wonder.

"Never mind!" snapped Marian. Madly, she searched Dasher's pockets, came up with a ring of keys. Norris stood, and in a moment she had removed the cuffs. He had Dasher's .45 in his fist when they heard the clump of Garvin's feet on the stairs.

He entered the room with a folded tarp under his arm. He dropped it to the floor and followed it down when Norris bashed his head with the butt of the gun.

There was no one in any of the rooms upstairs. Dasher's routine about the wife and kids was pure fiction. If there was a phone, they couldn't find it.

They were crossing the living room, on their way to inspect the garage, when Norris caught her arm.

"All right," he said, "how did you do it?"

She opened her purse and produced the combination lighter.

"To explode a single bullet," she said, "all it takes is a hammer and a firing pin. That's the lighter part, up here. Then you need a small, rifled barrel." She gave a yank and the lighter separated from the case. The barrel chamber became visible below the top edge of the case, and from it she removed the empty cartridge with her fingernail. "To cock the weapon, you press this innocent looking screw on the lighter. At the same time this little door slides back from the mouth of the barrel. From a distance you wouldn't notice the opening. And that's all there is to it." She assembled the gadget and dropped it into her purse.

"That's all there is to it," said Norris. "Simple. Open any pocketbook and you'll find one. No woman should travel without it. Listen, Marian, who are you anyway?"

"You know my name, Paul. Shall I spell it?"

"All right, then *what* are you?"

She looked at him and her eyes clouded. "Sometimes I don't know myself, Paul."

"Well, whatever you are, thanks!" He kissed her lightly. "My God, *now* I'm trembling, when it's all over."

"Is it?" She looked at him solemnly.

"Oh, c'mon!" he said. "Garvin'll sleep a long time. Let's go get the police!"

CHAPTER 14

"Well," said Sergeant Jasco, "I've heard some nuthouse stories, but this one's a dilly!" He shook his head. "You'd almost *have* to be telling the truth."

"Of course we're telling the truth!" Norris exploded. "If you'll go out there and investigate—"

"Out where?" said the Sergeant. "Do you have an address?" He was a big man and tall, in his trailing thirties. He had deliberate gray eyes and a hawk nose in a face which seemed overextended because of his high forehead and bald pate. He exuded the arrogance of petty power.

"No," said Norris. "As I told you, we never had the address. We were taken to the house by this man's chauffeur or whatever he is."

"We could show you the place," said Marian. She was seated in a chair beside Norris in front of the detective's desk. "I'm sure we could find it again," she added.

"When you came out of the house didn't you look for a number?" asked the Sergeant. His voice was accusing.

"Oh yes," said Norris. "But we couldn't find it."

The Sergeant raised eyebrows which were so blonde they were nearly invisible, underlining the naked impression of his features.

"You couldn't find it," he said. "And you can't even tell me the street."

"It was so dark," said Marian. "And of course we were shaken and in a hurry."

"All right," said the Sergeant, tapping a sheet of paper on which he had been writing certain information. "Now—this man Dasher threatened you with a gun. And when he did this, you, Miss, shot him. Is that right?"

"Yes."

The Sergeant's smile was depreciating. "How could you do that?

"I'd think he'd have been watching you every second."

"Well, he was. But then he turned away for just a moment. I had my hand in my purse as if to get a cigarette. I got the gun out and shot him."

"Dead?"

"I think so. He looked dead."

"And where is the gun now?"

"I—I dropped it. In the excitement."

"I see," Jasco did not see at all. His expression made it apparent.

Norris gave Marian a look. But her eyes were steadfast on the detective's. Well, he was certainly not going to contradict her story. Not now, anyway. She must have her reasons.

"Do you have a permit," said Jasco, "to carry such a concealed weapon?"

"No. But, my God, is that important right now!"

"That's true," said Norris. "We're wasting time, Sergeant."

"Look, mister," said Jasco, "I'll decide if we're wasting time and what's important here. I didn't make sergeant in this department by running off halfcocked. And I never run at all until I know where I'm going, and why."

"Sorry," said Norris. He wasn't really, though the man had a right to be slightly confused.

"Let's get on with it, then." Jasco plucked a pencil from behind his ear. He studied the paper. "Let's see. You're Norris and you flew out of New York with this lady, Miss Collison. What was your purpose in coming here?"

"Well, we—"

"We came to see this Gus Dasher," Marian interrupted. "We were sent by our company to investigate the financial and managerial status of the Morgan Van Lines office in San Diego. It's not public knowledge, but the San Diego branch of Morgan is failing and is secretly up for sale. Our company buys such firms and Mr. Kavanagh, the president, wanted us to bring back an opinion on the soundness of such a move, after a thorough study. Mr. Norris is an expert on these matters and I'm his assistant."

"Why doesn't Mr. Norris speak for himself?" Jasco inquired with a frown. "Is what the lady says correct, sir?"

Norris decided to play along for the present. "Yes," he said. "That's it. That's correct."

"In that case, where does Dasher fit?"

"He was supposed to be an efficiency expert," said Marian, before Norris could open his mouth. "He was supposed to have a complete file on the Morgan outfit. We were going to spend a couple of days with him first. You understand, a kind of orientation session."

The Sergeant did not understand any of this part, Norris observed. But he was loath to admit his ignorance of business, and for that very reason he asked no questions which might reveal him.

"Okay," he said. "That much is clear. Though why this guy would want to kill you beats me. Any idea?"

"None at all," said Marian.

Norris eyed her in amazement. Why was she protecting Kavanagh? He couldn't make a liar of her now. But later he would damn well find out.

"What about you, Mr. Norris? Any idea why this man would want to kill you?"

"No, sir. I can't think why."

"We'll find out," said Jasco sagely. "Now, when you left the house, you had the keys to this guy's station wagon. So you just got in and drove it off, is that it?"

"We had no transportation and we were in a hurry," said Norris, who resented the sergeant's tone of harping accusation about every detail. The man was a martinet; he had no imagination. "After all," he continued, "we could hardly ask permission."

Jasco played that one back and didn't like it. He seemed about to cut Norris down but couldn't find the words. Instead he reached into a drawer of the gray-steel desk and produced a phone book. He flipped pages and for some moments ran his index finger down columns.

"Nope," he said. "Can't find anyone by the name of Gus Dasher."

"We didn't see a phone," said Norris.

"These days, mister," said Jasco, "everyone has a phone."

"Not everyone," said Marian.

"Could be unlisted," said Norris.

"We'll check," said the Sergeant. He dialed and after a brief conversation, hung up. He shook his head. "Nothing doing. You know,

I'm beginning to wonder if there ever was anyone by the name of Gus Dasher."

"Are we making it all up, officer?" Marian asked wearily.

"You tell me, Miss. Are you?"

"That station wagon isn't made up out of vapor," said Norris.

"Where is the vehicle now?" Jasco asked with the air of one who might not even believe what he sees.

"Right out front," said Norris. "At the curb, you'll find the gray Chevy."

"It shouldn't be right out front," said the Sergeant. "Official vehicles only. No parking, day or night, in front of the station."

"Jesus!" said Norris.

"What's that?"

"I mean, Jesus, you're right. I don't know why I didn't think of it."

"Anyway," said Jasco, "we'll check that baby out with the registration bureau, then we'll just see. It'll take a little time, so why don't you folks just relax. You can sit here and talk it over. Maybe you'll come up with something else that makes better sense."

"We'll try," said Norris. "We'll really try."

"Pete!" the Sergeant called to a shirt-sleeved man at another desk. The two officers left the room.

As soon as they were gone, Norris said, "If that guy had to stop a gun fight in a bar and there was a hydrant in front, he'd park a block away."

"He's the ponderous type," said Marian. "His little mind is cluttered with details, memorized from the book. But I suppose he's doing the best he can. We must sound idiotic to him with our Edgar Allen Poe tale."

"Sure. And where did you get the one about our mission and Kavanagh? For God's sake, are you protecting him? After this?"

"Sorry if I confused you. I had to talk fast and all around you. But, Paul, listen to me. I've known Everett Kavanagh for years. No matter what Dasher said, he had nothing to do with this. I just don't believe it. Kavanagh is not a criminal, number one. Number two, he has no reason to want to get rid of us. What do we know? If we knew what was in the crate we might have cause to wonder. And three, even if by some thousand-to-one shot it was true that he sent us to a trap, how could we prove it? Who would take our word? Where's your evidence?"

"If Kavanagh didn't send us to a trap," said Norris, "then you tell me what actually did happen. There just isn't any other answer."

"There's one possibility," said Marian, "and I like it. Not Kavanagh, but someone else wanted to get rid of us. Someone who discovered where we were going and who we were to visit. So what does he do? Simple. He has an accomplice waylay the real Dasher's chauffeur and take his place. From there on it's no problem, because at the outset we're prepared to believe we're in the good old trusty hands of Dasher and company."

"My God, Marian, you may be right! I never thought of it."

"Yes," she said. "I'm sure that's what happened. Tomorrow we'll call Mr. Kavanagh and straighten it all out. I like to think we still have our jobs."

"I'm not so sure I want mine anymore. I've suddenly become disenchanted with the Kavanagh Company."

"Oh, stick around," she said, "for laughs."

"Yeah," he answered. "For laughs."

CHAPTER 15

After an age, Sergeant Jasco came back. "I had to wake a man up to get the information," he said. "Hell of a thing at this hour." He sat down and got a cigarette going. He leaned back, working his jaw. He seemed to enjoy keeping them waiting.

"Now," he said. "I think we've finally got the truth. The station wagon belongs to a Mrs. Elsie Dinsmore. She's a widow, elderly lady. Lives with a companion, name of Judith Tishler. Sometime last night the wagon was stolen from Mrs. Dinsmore's garage. She didn't even know it was gone until I called. She figures it was taken after they went to sleep. The two women were at home all evening, watching the TV."

He paused and looked from one to the other dramatically.

"All right. So far, so bad." He took a notebook from his pocket and flipped it open. "Mrs. Dinsmore and her friend live at 325 Ocean-cliff Road. The address is plainly marked above the mailbox beside the door. Mrs. Dinsmore and the Tishler woman have lived at that address for better than eleven years. It sounds like the same area you describe. But your story is full of holes. You're both lousy liars."

Norris looked at Marian and back to the sergeant. "You're being snowed, officer. All the way under. Let's go out there and we'll prove it."

"We'll go out there if and when I'm ready," Jasco snapped. "Meantime, I'll tell you what I think really happened. You people were loitering in that neighborhood and you wanted a car to go joy riding. You passed the Dinsmore place and you saw the garage door open, the wagon inside. It was late and the house was dark. You entered the garage, found the keys in the station wagon, and drove off.

"You had your fun, and when you got scared you might wind up in the pokey for car theft, you came on in here with your fairy tale. While you were at it you told a whopper. It was so fantastic I almost believed it. Why don't you admit it."

"That's the most ridiculous accusation I ever heard," Marian sputtered. She opened her purse and laid a roll of bills on the desk. "We've got hundreds of dollars with us, why on earth should we steal someone's car?"

Jasco eyed the money. "While we're at it," he said, "maybe we should find out how you got that dough."

Marian picked up the bills and put them away. "It's hopeless, Paul," she said. "Let him believe what he wants. Maybe we're safer in jail, anyway."

"No!" said Norris. "I want this thing investigated now, or they'll hear a noise from me all the way to the governor's mansion!"

The sergeant sighed. "I could lock you up until morning," he said. "But I'll give you a break, since you came in here on your own." He glanced at his watch. "It's twenty to five. Those poor old dames have gone back to bed. You can sit here until eight. Then we'll go out to the Dinsmore place and have a talk with the lady…"

* * * *

It all looked different in the daytime along Oceancliff Road. Innocuous. Peacefully suburban. Pastel houses overlooking a pastel ocean of pale green water gently combing a tidy shoreline. A tranquil place of *lazy* palms, of sun and sand, a place where evil seemed no more than a rumor in the morning newspaper.

Sergeant Jasco drove the station wagon. Another detective, the one Jasco had called "Pete," rode beside him; a small silent man with fat cheeks and a look of sober indifference behind hornrimmed glasses. Norris sat in back with Marian, trying to recall a dream of more shocking unreality than the past two days and nights.

It had been useless to argue with Jasco that this delay defeated the whole purpose of surprising the evidence which would verify their story. By this time Garvin must have awakened from his unwanted sleep with no more than a headache. And what of Dasher, that corpse in a basement room? Well, the room itself might have something to say. As for Dasher's crematorium, it could have been a sardonic joke. Though Norris didn't think so at all.

Jasco had sgrlowed down and was craning his neck out the window.

"This one here is three-twenty-one," he said. "Must be just a couple of houses down."

"Three-twenty-five, plain as your nose," said the officer called Pete, and Jasco swung into the drive.

"This is it," said Marian. "I'm sure! Look at the bay window, Paul, and the green shutters and the entranceway. And the two-car garage with the bouganvillae climbing over it. Yes, this it it!"

Jasco braked and turned around in his seat. "You agree, Norris? This it?"

"Looks a little different in daylight," said Norris. "But there's no doubt about it. This is the house."

"The murder house," said Jasco, smiling. "A pretty spooky place, eh, Pete?"

"Horrible," said Pete. "I'm really scared."

"Where's the murder car?" said Jasco with mock dismay. "Don't see it. You know, the big black limousine?"

Norris glanced at the garage. It stood gaping, empty. "It's gone," he said, "naturally. Did you expect the guy to wait for us?"

Jasco's smile faded. He got out and the three followed him to the door. There was a brass mailbox and just above it in dark green, the large plate numerals of the address. The sergeant tapped the numbers and gave Norris a meaningful look.

"Well," he said, "those numbers weren't there last night. I'm positive!"

Jasco rang, and in a moment a gray-haired lady near seventy opened the door. She was a tiny doll of a woman with parched skin, pale, bluish lips and crisp, brown eyes. She had a wart on one cheek; her hair was tied in a bun. She wore a dainty check apron with which she was wiping the food-flecked corners of her mouth.

"Oh," she said brightly, "you must be the police."

"That's right, ma'm. I'm Sergeant Jasco and this here is Detective Schoenberg. These other poeple, well, they're the ones who swiped your car."

The woman gave Norris and Marian a quick embarrassed glance before her eyes flicked back to the Sergeant. "We were just finishing breakfast," she said. "I'm Mrs. Dinsmore. Won't you all come in and have coffee?"

"No, ma'm, thank you. Just a fast look around, if you don't mind."

Norris recognized the living room instantly, remembered the two steps down to the oval space, with its maple pieces, and beyond the narrow hallway to the bedrooms.

"That brass lamp with the brass chain," said Marian, looking up to a ceiling fixture.

"Sure," said Norris. "Same one. It's all the same. This is the house."

"Mrs. Dinsmore," said Jasco in a courtroom voice. "Have these people, Mr. Norris and Miss Collison, ever been in your house before?"

Mrs. Dinsmore allowed her squinty eyes to settle upon the pair with nervous reluctance, while her little hands fluttered in the folds of the apron.

"No," she said with a small shake of her head, "I—I'm afraid not." She seemed genuinely disturbed.

Norris had not once taken his eyes from her face. She appeared to be nervous all right, even a bit frightened. But this could be the natural reaction of a timid person, unfamiliar with the law and its process, plus her obvious embarrassment in the role of the accuser. She had a soft, even kindly face, one which he could not picture hiding so great an evil. He was deeply puzzled.

"You have never," said Jasco dramatically, "seen this man and this woman before?"

"No, sir," she said. "Not ever, that I remember."

"So far, so bad," Jasco said. "And have you ever known or heard of anyone called Dasher? A Mr. Gus Dasher?"

"Never," said Mrs. Dinsmore.

"Or a Chuck Garvin, his chauffeur?"

"No," she said, "not him either. I'm afraid I just don't know what on earth this is all about." She stood blinking in the center of the room, turning from one face to another, seeking an answer.

"Of course not," said Jasco smugly. "We won't disturb you again if you'll just let us take a look at your basement."

"Basement?" she said with absolute bewilderment. "What basement? We don't have a basement here."

"It's off the kitchen," said Norris. "You go through the kitchen and turn to the right."

"Sure," said Jasco, "to the right." He made a wry face. "Do you mind, Mrs. Dinsmore? We have to humor the insane. Which way is the kitchen?"

"This way," she said, and beckoned them to follow.

Norris had given little attention to the kitchen. But he had noted that the walls were pale yellow, as indeed they still were.

At the left side of the room there was a dinette alcove. A table was set for two in this area, a clutter of dishes upon it. A woman sat facing them, munching a corner of toast. She was twice the size of Mrs. Dinsmore, a fat gray woman near the same age, with a fleshy face and docile eyes of pale blue. She shifted great varicose-veined legs beneath the table and smiled shyly when she was introduced as the companion, Judith Tishler.

"Now," said Jasco to Norris. "Which way to the basement? Show me."

Norris gazed at a door across the room.

"Over there," said Marian, pointing. "We went down over there."

Mrs. Dinsmore didn't get it. "Here?" she said. "Why this door is to a broom closet, that's all." She opened and they looked.

There was a broom, a dust pan, a mop and pail, aprons hanging from a hook, assorted empty pop bottles on the floor.

Norris stepped over and leaned inside. He felt around the interior. It was certainly just a closet, no more.

"This is a trick," he said. "One hell of a lousy trick! We went down to the basement right through this door. At least, it was just about here." He peered at the walls and saw nothing in the least suspicious. "You've got to believe us," he said. "We didn't make all that up. Somewhere down there you'll find a dead man, if you'll just listen. For God's sake, Sergeant, you've got to help us find that room!"

"They've covered it all up," said Marian. "Somehow they covered it all up."

"I've had enough," said Jasco. "Was there ever a basement in this house, Mrs. Dinsmore?"

"Oh, no," she said. "I've had this house eleven years, and I built it. There never was a basement. None of the houses around here have cellars."

"C'mon!" said Jasco, and strode out of the room.

At the door, he said, "I don't know what else these people are, Mrs. Dinsmore, but they're certainly liars, and they stole your wagon. So now, if you'll drive us to the station and sign a complaint, we can certainly get the D.A. to prosecute for auto theft."

"Well," said Mrs. Dinsmore, "I'd be happy to drive you all to the police station, of course, but I don't know about the rest. I really don't know." She studied Norris and Marian. "They look like such nice people. Confused perhaps, but not criminals."

"You meati," said the sergeant, "you want us to drop the whole thing?"

She took a breath, sighed. "Yes," she said. "Be a good man and let them go. We'll just say they *borrowed* my station wagon." She nodded. "Yes, they borrowed it, don't you think, Sergeant?"

"Well, I'll be a son of a—" Jasco glared. "I think you're making a mistake, ma'm." He turned to Norris and Marian. "I don't know what your game is," he said. "Either you're nuts or you're sharpies, con artists. We've got no record on you, so I'm gonna let you go. But you try one more little caper like this and you've had it, both of you. Now beat it!"

"Wait," said Mrs. Dinsmore. "We could at least drive them into town."

"Yes," said Norris dryly, "especially since our bags are in the station wagon, and I'm damn well not going to carry them two or three miles."

"That's true," said Marian. "We can't walk with the bags. But isn't the sergeant nice to set us free, after all we've done?"

CHAPTER 16

Norris crossed the room and looked down three stories upon the beach. Two blonde girls of five or six with identical swim suits piled sand on sand, erecting crude structures with gay little shovels. After a bit they tired and began to chase each other with toy pails full of salt water. At last, thoroughly drenched, they collapsed in front of their parents, giggling uncontrollably. The young man, who must have been the father, watched with a tolerant smile. The young woman in the yellow bathing suit rested her head on a folded towel and, yawning, stretched in the sun. Far out to the horizon, a ship smeared the sky with lazy plumes of smoke.

Norris turned his gaze back to the room and Marian Collison. She sat filing a nail and squinting at him with the sightless expression of one who looks inward for some misplaced knowledge, as a name on the tip of the tongue.

It was a big square room, high ceilinged, furnished incongruously with light wicker and heavy walnut. French doors opened onto a seaview balcony. The hotel was wood-framed and antiquated, though fresh from painting and well kept.

Riding back in the station wagon they had spied a motel near town. Norris had given Marian half a wink and asked Jasco to drop them there. It was a dodge to escape having the wrong people know the right address. Immediately they called a taxi and wheeled among the beach traps until they came upon this more remote, nondescript hotel. They had taken adjoining rooms and, after breakfasting in the musty coffee shop, had gone above to unpack. A minute ago he had knocked and Marian had opened the connecting door.

"I think we should call," said Marion now.

"Call who?"

"Who else?" Marian laid the file on an end table. "Mr. Kavanagh, of course." She examined the rebellious nail. "He should know about

Dasher, what there is to know."

"That's not much," said Norris, folding himself into a chair.

"And how does it tie in with his precious shipment—the awful box?"

"Why do you call it that?" She gave him a careful look.

"Because everything connected with it is a nightmare. It's also ridiculous, when you think that we could have died without ever really knowing why. If curiosity killed the cat, at least he didn't die still curious. Or did he?"

"I really ought to call Mr. Kavanagh," said Marian, retrieving the file, bending it this way and that.

"Yeah," said Norris, "so he can set up another firing squad—Dasher, Slasher, and Masher, murder by proxy."

"You have a weird sense of humor, Paul." Her lips twitched and her eyes smiled. "That little old woman, Mrs. Dinsmore, you know, I almost believed her. She seemed incapable. And, I don't know, sort of—"

"Guileless?"

"Yes. Exactly."

"I'll give you a guess, Marian. She knows a little, maybe, but not much. Not the truth. It's possible she really doesn't know the basement exists."

"She certainly had me convinced," said Marian. "For a moment there, I wasn't sure we were in the same house. Lord, what a creepy experience."

"Yes," said Norris. "On the surface. But underneath there's got to be a very sane explanation. You have to come back to the one basic, the one invariable—that station wagon. We drove it away from Dasher's house. It was in his possession. It leads to him directly."

"You're right, Paul. And forgetting the kitchen and the broom closet and Mrs. Dinsmore and her fat friend, I did remember that house. So what's the answer?"

"I can think of one," he said. "We know there definitely is a basement in that house. With a simple but clever rearrangement, the basement is concealed. Which makes Mrs. Dinsmore a liar. Or—she doesn't know the basement exists. Remember how quiet Dasher was until we went down there? He said the kids and wife were sleeping.

A lie, obviously, but someone could have been sleeping. How about trying Mrs. Dinsmore and her obese playmate for size? They could have been asleep in some little room we missed."

She nodded. "Maybe, but a little risky for someone of Dasher's cunning mentality. And at the very least, however innocent she was, Mrs. Dinsmore would have to know that Dasher was in the house for some reason or other."

"Well," said Norris, "however it appears, it's no spook problem. It'll make sense when we find out—if we find out. And if we don't, I'm not going to sleep too well."

"Why?" She brought out the ebony case and lighter, produced a cigarette.

"I'll tell you if you promise not to point that thing," he said.

She smiled. "It's not loaded." She gave herself a light. "Why, Paul? Why won't you sleep until you know about the house?"

"Because our friend Garvin is no ghost. He's alive and probably worried. He'll want to cover his tracks, and he'll be searching for us. He's just one guy, of course. But I have enough people to look for over my shoulder. Wheeler, for one, and those twin maniacs who probably murdered Taggart."

"I've simply got to call Mr. Kavanagh," said Marian.

"Oh, God," Norris moaned. "You have a sharp mind, really brilliant, but one track. Well, there's the phone."

He heard her talking to the operator, and then one of those protecting intermediaries through whom calls to Kavanagh flowed. And then to Kavanagh himself, speaking with a breathless urgency, explaining, explaining things he knew so well. But mostly she was listening and nodding with little gasps of surprise. Then she put down the receiver with the most astonished expression.

"Well?" Norris said.

"He's been trying to reach us, Mr. Kavanagh. He wanted to tell us that he's flying to Washington. It's something about this thing in the crate. We won't be able to contact him for a couple of days."

"All right," said Norris. "What's so startling about that?"

"Don't you see? He called us at Dasher's place. Naturally, he would. And Mrs. Dasher told him that her husband, Gus Dasher, is dead."

"That makes sense. We know he's dead."

"Yes. But he's *been* dead for three months. He died of a stroke. In a hospital up in L. A."

"No!" For God's sake, didn't Kavanagh just talk to him yesterday, when he made the arrangements for us?"

She shook her head. "That's just it. Mr. Kavanagh didn't talk to Dasher at all. Not personally. He was terribly busy and he had Miss Pelham, the new secretary outside his office take care of it. She simply reported that Mr. Dasher would be very happy to put us up for a few days. Actually Mr. Kavanagh had been out of touch with Dasher quite awhile."

"So where does that leave us?" said Norris.

"Well, it means that Miss Pelham was a kind of spy someone planted in the office."

"Was?"

She nodded. "Was. You see, she didn't come to work today, and when Mr. Kavanagh sent a man to trace her down, he found her missing from her apartment."

"Missing?"

"That's right," said Marian. "Packed up. Gone."

CHAPTER 17

"Then Kavanagh wasn't the one who set us up for the kill," Norris mused.

"Of course not." She said this absently, as if she had already begun to cope with a new problem.

"And what does Kavanagh want us to do now?"

"Nothing. I mean, nothing has changed."

"It hasn't?"

"In the plan, silly." She smiled broadly, and the effect was charming. "We're to go ahead with the same scheme to bring back the crate. I'm to remain here in the hotel, while you—"

"Rush down to San Diego in search of another way to get killed."

"Mr. Kavanagh said that if you wanted to quit, he wouldn't blame you. But if you are willing to stick with it and if you can get that crate back safely, there's a ten thousand dollar bonus."

"How much?"

"Ten." She held up both hands.

"Thousand?"

"Thousand." She got off the bed and came to him. She gave his cheek a little pat. "But," she said, looking up earnestly. "It isn't enough. No amount is enough. You ought to quit. Run fast and as far as you can go, before it's too late."

"Just forget Kavanagh and his old crate?"

"Yes." Her eyes were unsmiling. "Will you do that, Paul? For your own sake. Please?"

"And what about you?"

"Me? I'll just stay here until he sends someone to replace you."

"Why?"

"Because I'm committed. Call it anything you like: false loyalty, stubborn curiosity; or—maybe a certain rootless feeling I'd have without this job. But I'm going to hang on."

"So am I," he said. "I need the money, and I have my own root-less feeling. Risks don't bother me the way they might have once. Besides, what's the difference to you if it's me or some guy he sends as a replacement?"

She frowned, her eyes struggled with the answer. "Well," she said, "it wouldn't be so personal. I wouldn't get to know him or…like him."

He kissed her then. At first she was unresponsive. She didn't fight him. She simply stood there and accepted his lips. But after a moment her arms went around him, her mouth spread over his and with a shuddering sigh, she pressed against him.

He backed towards the bed and brought her down on top of him. With urgent fingers, she helped him remove the sweater and all beneath. But when he lay gasping in the turgid warmth of her breasts, his hand searching her thigh, she grew suddenly tense and resistant.

"Don't misunderstand, darling," she murmured. "I'm not one of those tease-and-duck phonies. I like you—maybe more. But right now I'd only be half a woman for you. And that half would be simply escaping."

"What's wrong with escape?" he urged.

"What's wrong with eating when you're really not hungry, just empty? Oh, Paul, Paul. Let's wait until it can be something better than a valve for tension. All right? Please understand. You'll have so much more of me if you wait."

This was always true. The best of a woman was offered in her own good time. "All right," he said. "But don't go away.

Just lie here beside me. Because I don't have the same set of brakes. And I'll have to coast to a stop."

She laughed and after a minute he got up and peered from the window while she adjusted her clothing. Then he crossed to the door. She came to him and when he had kissed her again, he went out.

The clerk at Morgan's warehouse in San Diego was a narrow young man with a narrow face and a neat mustache to match his dark hair. He had quick brown eyes and there was about him an air of alertness and good humor. He took the receipt from Norris and, after inspecting it, slowly shook his head.

"This here," he said, snapping the paper with a forefinger, "is routed to New York, my friend. Not San Diego."

"That's true," said Norris. "But at the last minute it was redirected."

"Well then," said the young man pleasantly, "they should have given you a new invoice."

"Don't I know it," said Norris, who had been expecting this. "Tell you what happened. This man who wrote up the papers was a bit put out with me for making the change. Can't really blame him. He got excited and gave me back the same slip. I didn't notice it until yesterday when I arrived. But then it was too late."

He frowned and tugged at the lobe of an ear. Suddenly he smiled. "Well, don't worry about it. We'll fix it somehow. Did you wanna pick this crate up or what?"

"Sure like to," said Norris. "Lot of junk in there the wife and I need to set up housekeeping. But it can't have arrived yet. Maybe you could tell me when it's expected, though."

"Okay," said the clerk. "Just have a seat. It's gonna take a little time."

"No hurry," said Norris and fell into a chair.

It was ten minutes before the clerk returned. "Nope," he said. "Nothing in the files on this one at all. Sure it was supposed to come here?"

"Positive. Is there any way you can check further?"

"No, sir, not at the moment. We could get a letter off to the Miami office tonight."

"I've got to know now," said Norris. "I'll be glad to pay for a call." He produced a ten dollar bill. "Here, you take this and if you can place the call at company expense, keep it anyway for your trouble."

The clerk folded the ten and stuck it in his pocket with a wink. "We'll find out," he said, "one way or another." He moved off purposefully.

Norris returned to his chair and this time had to wait even longer. His nerves tightened with each passing minute and when finally the clerk appeared, his expression did nothing to relieve the strain. The man looked puzzled and his face was shadowed with something like suspicion.

"How'd you make out?" said Norris breezily.

"Not good," said the clerk. "Not good at all. Strangest goddam thing I ever heard. Mister, are you by any chance with the police?"

"Maybe," said Norris cautiously. "Maybe not. We'll discuss that when you tell me what happened to the crate."

"Well, I suppose it's no secret," said the clerk. "Must of got in the papers back east."

"Oh yeah?" How come?"

"One of our vans," said the clerk, "was hijacked somewhere around Raleigh, North Carolina."

"No!" said Norris.

"Yup. And you know what they stole? Just one item." He tapped the receipt. "This crate. Not another thing but this here crate. That's why I thought maybe you were, well—"

"A cop?"

"Are you?"

Norris smiled, trying with difficulty to hide his amazement and his vast disappointment. All he wanted now was to get out of there quickly.

"You're pretty sharp," he said. "You came close. I'm an investigator for the party who owns the crate. We're working with the police, of course."

The clerk nodded. "Thought it was something like that. But what brings you out here to Dago? I don't see the connection."

"We got a tip," said Norris. "The crate was supposed to have been redirected here from Miami. But if the van was hijacked near Raleigh, the crate must have been on its way to New York."

"My God," said the clerk. "Too much for me. What's in that crate, anyway?"

"Sorry," said Norris, shaking his head and looking mysterious.

"Well, I'll tell you one thing for sure, mister."

"What's that?"

"If they stole it from Morgan and it's on its way here, it ain't comin' by one of *our* vans. That's for damn sure!" He offered a wry grin and took the folded ten from his pocket. "Here's your sawbuck, mister. I didn't need it."

"Keep it," said Norris. "I'll put it on the expense account. And thanks a lot, buddy."

He went out.

CHAPTER 18

In the phone booth Norris wedged the receiver in the crook of his shoulder and got the cigarette going. The hotel switchboard had been ringing Marian's room and, when she didn't answer, he had asked to have her paged.

He blew smoke at the busy toy fan overhead and tapped his foot with impatience. She had promised not to go out, though perhaps she was downstairs in one of the public rooms. Still, he had the uneasy feeling of new trouble forming like a big wave that was going to crash over him any minute. Nothing had gone as planned; the whole goddam deal was a crazy web of disaster.

"Sorry, sir," said the operator, "we are unable to locate Miss Collison. Would you like to leave a message?"

He said no, he would be there himself in an hour, and hung up.

He bought a paper and then he glanced around the drug store until he spied a booth that was vacant. When the waitress came he ordered coffee and a cheeseburger. He spread the paper on the table and began a search of captions and datelines. It was a San Diego paper and therefore might not carry one word about the peculiar holdup of a van in North Carolina, especially since that was now yesterday's news. Yet, this was a sheet which used many of the wire service fillers and by chance there might be a followup.

He turned the pages rapidly to the end, finding no mention of the episode. Now he went back and read the news casually, killing time as he waited for his order. His attention was caught by a small item on page four, New York dateline.

PARK MURDER-SUICIDE A MYSTERY

NEW YORK— The bodies of a man and woman identified as Harry Wheeler, 41, and Eileen Taggart, 29, were found in Central Park at dawn this morning. Police theorized that Wheeler strangled Miss Taggart after a lover's quarrel, then shot himself with a revolver found in his hand.

Mystery surrounded the tragedy when it was discovered that Miss Taggart had been dead at least twelve hours before Wheeler took his own life.

As of this moment little had been learned of Miss Taggart's recent activities. But Wheeler was employed by Everett Kavanagh of the Kavanagh Holding Company. He was in charge of Kavanagh's "private interests." Mr. Kavanagh was reported to be in Washington on business and could not be reached for further details. Of interest is the fact that Mr. Kavanagh's Manhattan apartment overlooks a section of the park near the death scene.

The bodies were found by Irving Goldsmith who lives in the neighborhood and was strolling with his dog. Mr. Goldsmith said that he first noticed…

* * * *

Norris put down the paper and stared thoughtfully into space.

God! What about that? Wheeler dead, too, and not by his own hand either. Quick justice for a double cross. And Eileen Taggart's body removed from the Fifth Avenue apartment and placed next to Wheeler's in a fake murder-suicide—a neat whitewash for Kavanagh.

One thing was quite certain. Kavanagh was not, never had been, confiding his troubles to the police. A man who could arrange that sort of cover for murder had to be playing ball with the underworld, had to be anything but what he claimed to be. And if you took it a step further…

He stood quickly and gathered the paper under his arm. As he stepped away from the table, he nearly collided with the waitress bringing his order.

"Say, don't you want this burger and coffee, mister?"

"If it's good, you eat it," he said. "I just lost my appetite."

He tossed a dollar on the table and strode to the door.

In ten minutes he had rented a new Pontiac sedan and was pushing north at the outskirts of San Diego. For a time he was caught in a snarl of traffic, but soon Route 101 stretched clear ahead and he tromped down on the accelerator.

Now and then he glanced tensely into the rear-view mirror. If he was right in his new estimation of the situation, there was more danger than ever. There was nothing now that could be done about the crate, and it should be forgotten in the need for mere self-preservation. If not for Marian, he would pass La Jolla in a burst of speed, shoving on to L. A. and a plane for somewhere, anywhere. But Marian had to be convinced that Kavanagh had only one intention from the beginning—to get rid of them as neatly and untraceably as possible. Yes, she had to be convinced. If he could find her…

A half dozen autos changed places behind him, all of them suspicious in his frame of mind. He leaned a heavy foot on the gas until they were anonymous specks. And when he made the turn to La Jolla, he was positive no one had followed.

He went immediately to his room and knocked on the connecting door. There was no answer. He gave the knob a twist and the door opened.

The room was immaculate. It wore the tidy face of vacancy. Frantically he pulled at drawers, inspected the closet, the bathroom. Not a remnant of her anywhere, not so much as the dying fragrance of her perfume lingered in the air.

He stared about the room hopelessly, a violent sense of doom pounding his heart. A gust of emptiness rushed upon him and suddenly he was aware that Marian Collison was important to him, and he was frightened for her.

He made a leap for his own room and wrenched the receiver from the phone. "Miss Marian Collison in 306!" He was almost shouting. "Has she checked out?"

"Just a moment, sir." In a weary voice, bored and mechanical, "Yes, sir. Miss Collison has checked out, that's correct."

"How long ago?"

"I couldn't say, sir. Would you like me to inquire?"

"No. Just tell me if she left a forwarding."

"No, sir, she didn't."

"How about a message? It would be in my box. Paul Norris, 307."

"One moment, sir."

There was a longer delay and then the girl said, "No, sir, I'm sorry. No message."

"Thank you." He cradled the receiver and, lighting a cigarette, fell heavily into a chair.

The God awful part of it was that he didn't have the vaguest idea of what to do next. He didn't know where to turn, and especially to whom. Kavanagh? Even if by some miracle the man could be located in Washington, Norris was sure that Kavanagh would be the very one behind Marian's disappearance. They had both been taken in by that quick-thinking gag about Miss Pelham being an office spy who arranged their end, then vanished. Was it a gag? There was one way to find out, one way to know the score for all time.

He looked at his watch. Twenty of six. In New York it would be twenty of nine and, of course, the office was closed. But maybe Miss Pelham had a home phone. Dam! He didn't know her first name… Yes, he did, too! Marian had spoken to her by given name just as they were leaving. What in *God's* name was it? Jane? Joy? Joyce! That was it.

He placed a person-to-person call for Joyce Pelham, New York City, asking the operator to check with information. No luck. She wasn't listed in Manhattan. He insisted they try the boroughs and, after an age, they located a Joyce Pelham in the Queens book. She lived in Kew Gardens. He told them to place the call. This particular Joyce Pelham was at home.

"Are you," he said, "the Miss Pelham who works for Mr. Everett Kavanagh?"

"That's right," she said. "I'm one of Mr. Kavanagh's secretaries. Who is this speaking?"

For a long moment he was unable to answer. "This is Paul Norris," he said finally. "Remember me? You arranged our plane reservations to L. A."

"Oh, yes, sir," she said. "Of course. You and Miss Collison. What can I do for you? Aren't you still out there in L. A.?"

"Yes," he said. "That's right. Still here in L. A." Obviously she didn't know they were to have gone on to La Jolla. "But I'm trying to locate Mr. Kavanagh."

"Well, he's gone to Washington on an important business matter, and I'm afraid he just didn't want anyone to disturb him there for the time being. I haven't the least idea where you could reach him. I expect he'll phone in tormorrow."

"I see. You're positive? I mean, he might have changed his plans. You were at the office today, weren't you?"

"Certainly, I was there when he left this morning."

"Is that so? Well, who took Miss Collison's call? She phoned Mr. Kavanagh around ten."

"She did? Well, let's see…. I could have been on my coffee break. Yes, that's it. Miss Arnold must have been at my desk."

"Sure. Well, okay. You haven't talked with Miss Collison at all since we left?"

"Why, no. Is there anything wrong?"

"No, everything's just great. And thanks very much."

"Shall I give Mr. Kavanagh a message if he phones in?"

"Message? Yeah. Tell him I've resigned as of now. Tell him Norris is playing on the other team. He'll understand. Bye."

CHAPTER 19

Norris could tell from those perfectly natural unhesitating answers that Miss Pelham had nothing to conceal. And more important, she had been right there at the office, while Kavanagh was lying. Accepting that much was a start. Kavanagh was a deadly enemy.

One thing was vaguely reassuring. There was no evidence that Marian had been forced to leave the hotel. Perhaps it was naive to assume that just because her room wasn't turned upside down with blood on the walls… Yes, it was naive. There were quieter ways. And there was his conviction, however unfounded, that she would have left him a note. No, she was in plenty of trouble. Who would help him find her? Sergeant Jasco? What a dirty laugh that would be.

Was there anything he could do? Anything? He sat for a long time, mulling it over, chain smoking. Darkness had clouded the sky outside his window before his thoughts had made a full circle, and he decided that there was only one thing to do—nothing. There would be a certain passive action in doing just nothing, because by now they must know where he was. Norris was still a threat to Kavanagh, and also Garvin. They would hunt him down. Sooner or later. Facing the door, watching and listening, he would wait. He would be ready; whoever came would be made to talk.

Such brave plans. Yet, he was afraid.

He got up and gave the room light, crossed to the bed. He lifted the cover and heaved the mattress, reaching beneath. The gun—Garvin's .45—was still there. He had decided not to turn the gun over to Jasco. The sergeant would probably arrest him for carrying a concealed weapon. He didn't want to tote the big automatic around, and Marian had suggested the mattress.

His hand gripped the butt and yanked the weapon from its hiding place. Right away he saw the little scrap of paper fastened to the barrel with a rubber band. With anxious fingers he got the paper free and opened it.

There was nothing on it but an address scrawled in pencil. 937 *Oceancliff Road.*

The writing was hardly legible, written with hysterical haste, but it was Marian's hand. It must be! What did it mean? First, that she didn't want anyone else to find the paper in his room. Second, that he should go to the address. And third, perhaps that he should come armed.

He inspected the gun. The clip was full. He worked a bullet into the chamber and pressed the safety. He put the weapon in his hip pocket and flew out the door.

Downstairs he asked at the desk to see the registration cards which he and Marian had filled out that morning. He was brusque and his manner allowed for no questioning. When he had Marian's card in his hand he compared her script to the scrawl on the paper. Conceding that she had been nervous in one instance, calm in another, the writing was almost identical.

Outside he looked around carefully. He saw no one in the shadows by his car. Still, he checked the back seat before he drove off. He watched the mirror and, after a while, there did seem to be a car on his tail. The car followed at a leisurely pace—which proved exactly nothing. In a moment he veered sharply into a side street and parked. Lights out he waited, the gun in his hand. The dark shadow of a big sedan slid past the turn and vanished. He pulled the headlight switch and wheeled on, returning to the street which would lead him to Oceancliff Road.

Oceancliff Road—significant, but puzzling. The other address, of Mrs. Dinsmore and the hidden basement, was number 325. How did that house link with 937? Perhaps it didn't. He shrugged.

Automatically, he began to search for the white, frame facade of the Dinsmore woman's place. He found it easily enough, coasting past, straining to see. The living room was well lighted, the curtains open. He had a quick glimpse of the two old ladies, the backs of their gray heads visible as they viewed the flickering images on a television screen gesturing across the room. How innocuous was that little scene. How banal. How lacking in the least of sinsiter elements.

He counted the blocks to the nine hundreds, knowing they should begin about six blocks from the Dinsmore place. Then he slowed and, keeping at an even, unsuspicious speed, peered obliquely at the houses, not actually turning his head. He could see it was going to be difficult. He couldn't make out a single number. He would have to swing back and approach from the other direction, perhaps giving himself away.

He slid past another of those vacant lots, this one large enough to accommodate three houses. Then there was a white, frame house of the Cape Cod design and the instant he got a decent look at it he knew he had found 937. It was the exact twin of 325, the Dinsmore place. There was no further need to speculate upon the missing basement. How simple! So simple, it escaped all those complicated deductions. Two identical—one had a basement, one did not.

He went on by. There was another lot beyond. On either side the house was flanked by empty lots. Norris had a hunch that Dasher had owned both lots. With good reason, they had not been sold.

Norris went down the road and circled back. He parked off the pavement on the lot, approaching the area without lights. As on the first night of their arrival, a dim glow from the living room splayed on the lawn. Behind the heavy pistol, he crept around to the rear, pausing now and then to adjust to the darkness and peer about him. At the east extreme of the lot there was a mild cliff. Below was the white ribbon of a beach, retaining the minor undulations of a tranquil sea, and distantly, the pale carnival of lights from a seemingly motionless ship.

There was a tall hedge which screened the backyard. Norris parted the tangle and looked upon the darkened rear of the house. He watched and listened. After a time, he stepped onto the back lawn, crouching forward. The hard cool feel of the gun in his hand, his fingers ready at the trigger, he made his way to the back door. It was locked. But a screened window was open at the other end of the house, and, after listening with an ear against the mesh, he poked the barrel of his ballpoint through to the catch and released it. Soft as a feather, he climbed inside.

He was in a bedroom. Again his eyes adjusted and, when he could see that he was alone in the room, he became fascinated by the faint flush of light from beneath the door. He went forward and turned the knob, peering out cautiously.

That familiar living room! Empty. The silence of desertion. A single lamp burning, as if the family had gone to the movies, leaving this one warm signal for their return.

Norris crossed the living room nimbly, toward the kitchen with its yellow walls. He opened the door leading to a stairway caught in silhouettes by a distant light. And with the light, the sound of voices.

CHAPTER 20

Norris went down a step and closed the door softly behind him. He leaned against the wall, breathing deeply in a soundless rhythm, listening. There were several voices, one dominant above the rest. The words were lost in the hollow chambers of the basement. At times they had an alien quality, a strangeness that seemed unworldly.

There was a hush and this was followed by the echo of a tiny explosion. Then a quick-rising murmur, as if in approval. And at that moment Norris had the feeling that he was coming to the end of a long chain of evil which led to the room below.

He tiptoed down the stairs, testing each one for a giveaway signal of creaking wood. He held the gun before him, cherishing it as his only friend. He reached the cement floor and turned towards the light. It came from an open doorway to the left, apparently the same door-way which led to Dasher's "play room." He crept towards the room, keeping to the darkness beyond the area of light. The voices grew in volume, and now he could distinguish words, though he was unable to concentrate in the effort for concealment.

The passage was wide and it was possible to come abreast of the doorway and remain in the shadows by hugging the opposite wall. In any case the advantage was his, since, unlike those in the room, he could peer from darkness into light.

Now he gave his back to the wall and holding the .45 cocked and ready, blinked his eyes and stared directly into the room. All that it contained, except for a small portion to the right of the door, became visible. Whatever the hazy picture sketched by his imagination, it was far from close to the scene in that room.

A long oval mahogany table had been placed in the middle of the room, and over this table a cloth had been spread. At the center of the table rested a frosty bucket. And from the bucket protruded the neck of an open magnum of champagne. It came to Norris with some small sense of chagrin that the weird little echo, the tiny explosion, had been caused by no more than the hollow pop of a cork removed from a bottle. But the rest of the picture was so really incongruous that he quickly forgave himself.

There were four people at the table, each holding a glass of champagne, each wearing a somewhat similar expression of smug pride, as if in the celebration of some momentous event just concluded against impossible odds.

The most prominent of these, sitting at the head of the table and facing Norris, was Everett T. Kavanagh. His black hair was combed with casual neatness, his bushy brows were slightly raised above dark eyes in deep sockets, still cool and placid as mountain lakes in winter. He spoke softly to the others, though his voice sang with a clarity and distinction that might have silenced a first-night audience of sneering sophistication.

These others to whom he spoke were, on his left, Marian Collison, and on his right, two white-clad naval officers who wore the gold stripes of command. These officers had strong jaws and ruddy faces, their features hewn from some Nordic or Germanic stock. They had removed their caps, revealing blonde heads with identical brush cuts. Despite the uniforms, Norris recognized them immediately.

At the end of the table opposite Kavanagh, there was a single empty chair and before it, an empty glass.

Marian Collison wore her burnt-orange dress, the one which clung to the graceful abundance of her figure. Her hair had the shine of devoted brushing, her makeup the subtlety of careful attention. She sat easily in her chair, her features relaxed, a piquant little smile on her face, the smile of a woman who knows she is attractive and has a captive all male audience. Taking dainty sips of champagne from her glass, she watched Kavanagh, her expression wide-eyed, enraptured.

There were two other persons in the room. These were sailors in full uniform. They stood at attention against the left wall and wore sidearms in dark leather holsters. Neither was tall, but both were stocky with hard muscles and hard faces. They had a still more alien look than the two officers, though their meaty features lacked the same refinement.

The sailors were separated by a large wooden box which came to their shoulders and sat squarely between them. Just beyond the box, towards the doorway, there was an orderly pile of heavy wood slats and odd sections of boards, as if the box had been recently uncrated on the spot.

There was nothing remarkable about the box itself. It was constructed of a sturdy, unpainted wood, was square in shape and apparently had a hinged door which was fastened by a simple catch. Yet the rigid stance and watchful expressions of the guarding sailors belied the commonplace.

Norris absorbed most of this in a single glance of astonishment, then studied the components of the scene in a rapid appraisal. Smiling, politely sipping their champagne, they were such a convivial group that Norris had a queer thought. Supposing, that after these trials and dangers, all had now been accomplished. And then suppose that with the help of Marian they had played a little gag on him. Gun in hand, prepared for anything, he would stride into that room and at the sight of him they would burst forth with laughter. After which they would riase their glasses and toast him for his part in the whole adventure. It did not seem so very absurd until he began to listen closely to the conversation.

"… No," said Kavanagh. "You still don't understand my reasoning." He smiled at Marian, the smile benign, yet also patronizing, then addressed the group in general. "You see, there is never a shred of wisdom in taking the least chance which can be avoided. Naturally, I might have allowed the crate to be transported to New York where I could have recovered it under normal circumstances, using the invoice which Norris unwittingly carried for our late friend Wheeler. But—and this is an enormous qualification—there was the risk that somehow the knowledge of the crate and its contents, had passed to the police. How? By Norris, of course. Was there a guarantee that he had told no one, regardless of anything he said?"

"Yes," said Marian Collison. "But the poor dope didn't have the first idea of what was in the crate. So therefore he had nothing to tell."

"Is that so?" said Kavanagh. He made a sneering face. "How can you be positive that our other dear departed Eileen Taggart, didn't give him the information?"

"Well, positive is too strong a word, Everett," said Marian. "But it seems perfectly logical that she had nothing to gain by telling and everything to lose."

"Now you listen," said Kavanagh, aiming a manicured finger at her, "listen and remember." His face was stern, almost menacing. "There is no such thing in our language as a word that is too strong—like positive!" He sat back and eyed them all. "No," he continued, "we must *always* be positive. Guesswork, uncertainty, carelessness, lie behind all the stupidity, all the failure in this most gullible of worlds."

"I'm sorry, Everett," said Marian meekly. "You're right. I just thought it wasn't logical for Eileen Taggart to—"

"Logic was not enough," interrupted Kavanagh, tasting his champagne with a modest smacking of his thin lips, while the two officers watched and listened with respect and also with a certain detachment. "Mere logic," he went on, "leaves margin for error. I have to be absolutely certain, because if a man like Norris had even an inkling, we would have been lost. We would have been met at Morgan's New York warehouse by a small army of tin cops in plainclothes. So it was necessary to have the van located and robbed of what was ours to begin with."

"Yes," said the officer closest to Kavanagh, "a smart move. I agree." He spoke with the barest hint of an accent, though correctly, without the foreigner's inversion of grammar.

German, Norris decided. They're all Germans.

"I'm glad to hear that you agree, Captain," said Kavanagh with a thin smile, "because it's just a little late to try it the other way."

"However," said the captain with a show of irritation, "I wish you had kept Norris in New York. We would have finished him off in short order if we had been given a chance. As it is, your man Dasher, or Dinsmore, if you like, bungled the job and got himself shot dead in the effort."

"Sure," said the second officer with a sour grin. "You bet. We would have closed his fat mouth in a big hurry. Goddamn right." He spoke with even less of an accent.

Kavanagh lit a cigarette and directed the smoke at the neck of the champagne magnum. "You boys had your chance," he said. "And there was already one corpse too many to accuse me in *my* city, near *my* apartment. You'll forgive me, but I think you handled the Taggart and Wheeler demise rather crudely. Especially the Taggart woman. Know what I mean? For that reason, I wanted Norris erased out here. Dasher was, in the past, terribly efficient. And his method was so utterly neat and evidence-consuming. Not a trace. No, I had the right idea. But I'm afraid Marian got panicky, didn't you, Marian?"

"Wouldn't you?" she answered with some defiance. "After all, I thought he was going to kill me—at *your* command."

"My dear girl," said Kavanagh. "You should know me better than that. My instructions were to scare you into permanent silence, not shoot you into permanent sleep. Then Dasher was to hold you here for my arrival and our little trip to Mexico."

"Did I need that much of a scare, Everett?"

He shrugged. "It's difficult to trust anyone in this business. Even you, Marian, in spite of my special affection for you. It just happened that you opened the wrong piece of mail. I told you that anything with a German postmark should never, never be touched by anyone but me."

"It was one silly mistake in a busy day," said Marian. "Besides, I don't read German."

"Can you prove that you don't?"

"Can you prove that I do?" She smiled.

"Well," he said, smiling himself, "it doesn't matter. We have no more secrets. You know them all."

"If that's a compliment," she said, "I'm grateful. But worried. I don't like to know too much. I can't forget Dasher."

"Such a clever gadget," said Kavanagh, taking Marian's deadly case and lighter from his pocket and weighing it in his palm.

"Ingenious," said the captain.

"I wish I had a dozen," said the other officer. "You bet."

"My husband was a gunsmith," said Marian. "Did I tell you? He liked to tinker in his spare time. He was always inventing lethal toys. That was one of them. Unfortunately it was a gun accident which killed him," she said sadly.

"Well," said Kavanagh, dropping the case into his pocket, "we'll discuss these personal items in Mexico, eh, Marian? Perhaps on the beach at Acapulco, after this business is concluded. But let's not bore our friends."

"Oh, I'm quite amused," said the captain, looking at his watch, frowning.

"Plenty of time," said Kavanagh. "We have nearly an hour."

"What about Norris?" said the captain.

"Don't worry," said Kavanagh. "You'll have him, one way or another."

"Regardless," said the captain, glancing again at his watch, "we leave at nine. After that he's your problem."

"Don't worry," said Kavanagh.

And precisely at that moment Norris stepped into the room and leveled the automatic.

"I wouldn't want you to worry about me, Kavanagh," said Norris. "So here I am."

Kavanagh seemed undisturbed. His face lost none of its blandness, his eyes, if anything, were colder than before.

"You're a little late," he said. "But not too late, Mr. Norris. Not too late."

"I want to see all your hands on the table," said Norris. "Empty. That means you too, Marian. You sailors over there, turn around and lean on the wall, then open your belts and drop your guns to the floor. Now!"

"It's useless," said Kavanagh. "They don't speak a word of English."

"Tell them," said Norris to the captain. "I'll shoot the first man who makes a wrong move."

From the corner of his eye, Norris watched the sailors, feeling within himself a small center of calm. The calm which comes with action after long waiting in fear. The sailors stood rigidly unmoving, only their eyes betraying awareness.

Now, for a fleeting moment, Norris looked directly at Marian. Her face was a blank. Her eyes were faintly disdainful. As yet, not a hand had appeared on the table surface.

"Captain!" Norris shouted. "I want those men to drop their guns, and I want to see hands on this table."

"You know," said the captain mildly, "my men would die before they would disobey an order. I have many orders. Some of them have been given already."

"I believe it," said Norris. "And I have a feeling that your men are going to die before they can reach those guns." He meant it. If necessary, he was ready to shoot down everyone in the room.

"Well," said the captain, rubbing the side of his nose with a forefinger, "I am sure you would kill my men before they could reach their guns. But you have another problem, my friend. You see, my brother and I are also wearing sidearms. Good German Lugers. The finest. Is that not so, Ernst?"

"That is so," said Ernst, nodding. "They are excellent weapons, precision made. We Germans have a special skill with arms. You bet."

"It is only because we are seated," said the Captain, "that you cannot see these fine guns."

It was true. The weapons could rest on their opposite hips, impossible to see. Norris had a hunch they were not bluffing. He was worried. There were too many guns in the room, everyone was too calm. They had been expecting him and there was a plan. Such a plan, carefully arranged, would certainly work. And now he had the feeling of disaster!

"All right," he said. "You might kill me, in the end, but just remember this. I'm not the only one in this room who will die. Kavanagh, you'll be first." He turned the barrel directly upon Kavanagh.

"I'll tell you, Captain Krauss," said Kavanagh. "This man is dangerous. And what's more, I believe he thinks you are bluffing him. Now it would be foolish to bluff a man with a weapon so powerfully destructive as a .45 automatic. A gun which repeats and repeats, firing again and again with the slightest touch of a finger. So I suggest that you turn at least one of those Lugers over to me so that I may prove to Mr. Norris your sincerity."

"Certainly," said the Captain. "You are welcome to show him my very own pistol."

And with a quick, extremely deft movement, Captain Krauss had passed a Luger across the table, butt first. So that in a second, Kavanagh held the weapon trained on Norris, the long barrel seeking his chest.

And that was when Norris pulled the trigger and shot Kavanagh at a range of ten feet. At least that was his clear intention. But when he pressed the trigger, there was only the thin sound of the hammer falling. After he had tried again several times and the laughter had subsided, Marian still giggling and wiping her eyes, Kavanagh said, "Did you think we would let you walk in here with a functioning gun and shoot even one of us? If there was ever going to be a next time, I would advise you to check your firing pin. Now drop that useless metal and sit down. Join the party. It's in your honor, my boy. Thank Marian. Most of it was her idea."

"Didn't I tell you he'd come?" said Marian. "Men are little boys. They like to play hero. Save the fair maiden in distress."

"Oh sure, sure," said Kavanagh, as Norris threw the gun on the floor disgustedly and sat down in the one vacant chair. "You were right, Marian. You were right."

"Anyway," said Captain Krauss, "he wouldn't have escaped. I'll bet Garvin never let him out of sight."

"Garvin is most reliable," said Ernst, "and he has a bump on his head that is aching for revenge."

Kavanagh set the Luger on the table. "Norris," he said. "Have you ever considered the glorious advantages of travel? No? Well, you have a voyage in store for you. You sail at nine. And though you'll never go anywhere but down, half the fun is getting there, as they say in the ads. But we have forty minutes to celebrate and talk of other things. We are not cruel, you know. We are not savages. It's all a matter of expediency, nothing personal. Now have some champagne." He took hold of the bottle and poured it into the one empty glass, sending it around to him full via Ernst. "Drink up!" he said, and all raised their glasses but Norris.

"I suppose," said Kavanagh, resting his hand on the Luger, "that you have a certain natural curiosity about the box." All turned with him to look upon it with awe. "I imagine that by this time you have conjured up some strange images. Now what do you think this box contains?"

"I don't give a godam what's in your box," Norris snarled.

"Not at all," said Kavanagh. "You are wondering. You have never stopped wondering. Now what do you say? I'll tell you, Norris. If you can guess, we'll give you a twenty-minute start. You have my word on it."

"How generous," said Norris.

"You won't even guess? I'm afraid, however, that you are going to be disappointed. Because you see, there is nothing at all in that box but paper." He formed a steeple of pale fingers and looked bemused. "Just paper. But oh, what paper it is! Shall we have a look?"

He winked at Captain Krauss and the captain barked in German at the guardian sailors. Whereupon the sailors turned immediately and fussed with the door of the crate, swinging it open.

Inside there was an enormous gray, metal box, similar in size to an overlarge steamer trunk. There were locks at either end of the box and these were opened by apparently unmatching keys which the sailors wore on chains around their necks. Now the sailors waited at strict attention. The captain barked another guttural command and instantly they lifted the cover.

The box was filled to the brim with tightly packed currency. A green horde of it so overwhelming that Norris could not conceive of the amount.

"How much?" said Kavanagh. "If you can guess, I'll give you five minutes to run." He chuckled. "Five!" That's the figure. Five million dollars in fifties and hundreds. Look it over, Norris. Go ahead! Walk up to it. Pick up a bundle, examine it."

Any action was better than sitting, so Norris obeyed. He went to the box and plucked a banded wad of hundreds. The bills showed medium usage and had a look of grand power, though at the moment he was not exactly excited by them. He inspected a larger sandwich of fifties with the same reaction.

"I have one more note of interest," said Kavanagh dramatically from across the room. He paused, then toyed with each word as he said, "Not one of those bills in the entire five million is genuine. Not one! And yet, in all history, they are probably the finest counterfeits ever created. Do you know why? Because they were made during the war by the German Government itself, using their most skilled engravers. The plates were seven months in the making. A perfect duplication of the paper used for our currency took even longer."

Norris said nothing. He thought of nothing but the fragmentary idea which was building in his mind. It was important for him to remain standing so he picked up another bundle of bills and flipped through them. They seemed flawless. In spite of himself he was amazed.

"When the job was completed," Kavanagh continued, "a test was made. A few bills were sent to this country where they were taken to several banks. The banks were told the bills were suspected of being counterfeit and the agents asked for a check. Each bank returned the bills after a day or two with the report that they were absolutely genuine.

"The plan was to finance Gestapo operations in the United States. A few traitorous American informers, spies and the like, had already been paid in the bogus currency. But of course the big scheme was to undermine the nation's economy with this avalanche of counterfeits. So, in order to manufacture the bills in quantity, a plant was set up under the supervision of an officer from the Reich Security Office, a special section. All was going well, millions had been printed and stored in secret caches, when the war ended.

"Now, the plates and some of this fake money were found at the bottom of a lake by the United States. And a great part of it was never found because it was hidden elsewhere. But the only surviving officer of that phony printing plant operation knew exactly where it was. And because I was notorious in certain limited quarters for black market and other profitable deals, it happened that an emissary from this officer got in touch with me and we came to terms. The bills you see there comprise the last of several shipments over the years. We had to be extremely careful. And, in fact, the situation is becoming a little too warm in the United States, and so we are going to distribute a large part of this Third Reich endowment in cheerful old Mexico."

"Interesting," said Norris, "at any other time. Right now I'm more concerned with my own welfare." With his thumb he flipped the bills like a deck of cards. "What's going to happen to me?"

"You," said Kavanagh, reaching for his champagne glass, "are going for a cruise to some remote and extremely deep area of the Pacific where you will be placed in a weighted box similar to the metal trunk which holds those bills and dropped overboard. Simple and effective. Though I liked Dasher's method better. His real name was Dinsmore, you know. His little old mother lives just a few blocks away in a house that's a replica of this one, an idea which has had its uses from time to time. She's a charming woman and has a deceptively innocent face."

Kavanagh swallowed and set down the glass.

"Actually, I bought both houses and installed Dasher, as we called him, in this one. Certain freighters, like the one captained by Krauss here, would anchor a few miles off the coast from this spot and of course they would be carrying various fascinating items. And they would send a boat ashore with these items, pick up their payment and depart forthwith. Captain Krauss is expecting a boat to come ashore for him at nine, and then he will take you to your destination. The captain has been hauling cargo around the world, more or less. And he would have been parked off the coast of Florida and it would have been much more convenient for us to take possession of the currency there. But the Florida coast is being watched, especially because of the arms running to Cuba, and the captain had to fly the box to Miami. Then we decided on Mexico for distribution and after a long foul-up because of Wheeler and so on, so here we are back again. But it turned out all right, didn't it?"

"What?" said Norris, who was looking at Marian. "Oh yes, great. It turned out just fine." He kept watching Marian, whose hand had moved along the table to creep slyly over Kavanagh's and squeeze. Norris looked her in the eye and said, "You bitch. You disgusting bitch."

Kavanagh scowled, but Marian only smiled and squeezed the hand tighter. It was the hand which lay on the table next to the Luger, and Norris wondered if he could grab it in time. No, it would never work. The sailors would shoot him, or Ernst would get him before he reachd the table. He could think of only one possibility, and there was never a better time.

The two sailors were standing at attention in front of the box and he walked between them, tossing the stack of bills carelessly on top of the others. As he turned back, he leaped behind the nearest sailor and threw a mighty strangle hold around his neck. Gasping and wretching, the sailor tried with both hands to pry the arm from his throat. That was when Norris got the Luger from the holster, keeping the sailor in front of him for a shield.

Meanwhile, the other sailor had drawn his pistol, but seemed to be waiting for an order, glancing at the captain from the corner of his eye.

"You're gonna have to shoot the sailor before you get me," said Norris, "so think fast and don't make a move." He held the gun directly on Kavanagh, ignoring the hesitant gob with the drawn Luger. Kavanagh seemed reluctant to reach for the weapon on the table. The story was a little different now.

"You know," said Captain Krauss, who was the coolest one in the room, "if I order that man to fire, he will. And a bullet can pass through two bodies almost as easily as one."

Norris looked at the other sailor, who stood with the Luger aimed directly at his buddy's midsection. "I don't think you'll order your own man killed, Captain," he said.

"Is that right?" said the Captain. "You are mistaken." He murmured something in German to the sailor and Norris tightened the strangle hold and pulled the other man back with him so that they rested together against the wall.

"You see," said Norris, when there was no shot, "you were bluffing, Captain. And that puts me in charge here."

"Do you know what I told the sailor?" said the Captain. "I told him to be ready to fire at my command. Just one word, and I'm prepared to say it."

"I'll never drop this gun and you know it, Captain," said Norris.

The captain stared at him for a long moment, then nodded. "It's true," he said philosophically. "You'll never drop the gun."

He turned to the sailor. His eyes grew wide and bright. *"Feuer!"* he shouted.

The Luger in the sailor's hand bucked, and there was the hollow pound of the explosion in the basement room. Norris felt the slug knife his chest with a searing pain at the same moment the man sagged, dead in his arms.

It should have been enough that he was alive, that the slug must have been deflected by a bone in the sailor's body, losing its force. But then, as the captain shouted, "Feuer!" again, it was Marian who obeyed the command first. She had picked up the Luger from the table and shot the second guard in the throat, so that he fell in a gush of blood.

It should have been over then. But Ernst snaked his gun from beneath the table, and Kavanagh began to grapple with Marian. Norris shot Ernst twice, once through the head. He had been half standing and he fell like a meal sack into the chair and toppled over backwards.

Kavanagh had Marian's gun arm, trying to twist her wrist. He did. But in the effort, he got the barrel of the Luger turned into his face for one instant, and in that instant, she pulled the trigger. The bullet drilled teeth, went through the roof of his mouth and out the back of his head.

Apparently the captain was the only survivor, and when he came up from the floor with the Luger taken from the dead hand of his brother, Marian and Norris fired simultaneously.

The room was a slaughter house, and after Marian had really seen it, she half-whispered, "Dead. They're all dead." She dropped the Luger as if it were some loathsome reptile and began to sob. She stopped abruptly, gave one more gasp and looked up at him. "You're bleeding," she said.

"I know. It's not serious."

"It wasn't supposed to happen this way," she said. "It was arranged to take them prisoner at nine when we all went down to the beach."

"Jesus, what are you talking about?" said Norris, who was shaking visibly.

"I had to make it look good," she continued. "I had to suggest luring you here and sending you off on the ship, or they would have had Garvin kill you in the room."

"Who are you, Marian? I'm going to ask that again. Who are you?"

"My husband worked for the Secret Service," she said. "He was killed trying to trace this cointerfeit money. That was years ago. They had just a small lead to Kavanagh and I offered to apply for a job with his company and get close to him. Of course, I wanted revenge. I've never been out of touch with the Secret Service. Their men should be down on that beach right now, and they should be holding Garvin because they knew he would be stationed outside."

"C'mon," said Norris. "Let's go see!"

On the back lawn the night washed them with its cool briny air. They paused a moment, breathing deeply, gazing at the dim distant lights of the ship which Norris had seen as he crept toward the house.

The ship remained fixed as ever on the horizon.

They went down the narrow stairs to the beach. They didn't see or hear anything until two men sprang from the darkness with drawn .38s.

"It's Marian Collison," she said in a voice edged with hysteria, "and Paul Norris."

"What the hell?" said one of the men, lowering his gun. "Where's Kavanagh and his sailors? I thought they were coming down at nine. We have a beautiful reception ready here, eight more men in hiding."

"You're a little late," said Norris. "They're all dead."

Marian explained. "What about Garvin?" she asked.

"We've got him in one of the cars above."

"Didn't you hear shots?" said Norris.

"Not a sound," said the officer.

"Well, anyway, it's over." Norris sighed.

"Except for that boat," said Marian, "coming to get the captain." She shuddered.

"We'll watch for it," said the officer.

They went back up the stairs and stood looking out to sea.

"What do you do when people are dead?" said Marian. "And you killed them?"

"You remember that they would have killed you first. Then you go back to the hotel and you sit in the bar and you have a drink. A lot of drinks. And you talk of other things, and you try to forget."

"I'm ready," she said.

And they moved off slowly to the car.

ABOUT THE AUTHOR

Robert Colby once said: "I began writing while in the South Pacific, invading Jap-held islands with the Army Infantry during World War II. After the war I wrote hit-or-miss for a year or two, then began to study, take private lessons, and attend creative writing courses. I wrote on-and-off for about seven years before I sold my first story to a magazine that promptly collapsed just after sending me a check!

"I then began to write novels and made my first sale, a novel, to Ace Books. Meanwhile, I held down a radio and TV announcer's job at various stations around the country—NBC in New York, CBS in Hollywood, KOA in Denver, WBEN in Buffalo, and WAVE in Louisville, to name a few. Most of the time I would announce half the night and write all the next day."

www.ingramcontent.com/pod-product-compliance
Lightning Source LLC
Chambersburg PA
CBHW020151180626
46810CB00004B/1832